# The Interspecies Poker Tournament

## The Roshaven Case Files No. 27

## Claire Buss

**Other works by Claire Buss:**

**The Gaia Collection**
The Gaia Effect
The Gaia Project
The Gaia Solution

**The Roshaven Books**
The Rose Thief
The Interspecies Poker Tournament – The Roshaven Case Files No. 27
Ye Olde Magick Shoppe

**Poetry**
Little Book of Verse, Book 1 of the Little Book Series
Little Book of Spring, Book 2 of the Little Book Series
Little Book of Summer, Book 3 of the Little Book Series
Spooky Little Book, Book 4 of the Little Book Series
Little Book of Winter, Book 5 of the Little Book Series

**Short Story Collections**
Tales from Suburbia
Tales from the Seaside
The Blue Serpent & other tales
Flashing Here and There

**Anthologies**
Underground Scratchings, Tales from the Underground anthology
Patient Data, The Quantum Soul anthology
A Badger Christmas Carol, The Sparkly Badgers' Christmas Anthology
Dress Like An Animal, Haunted: The Sparkly Badgers' Halloween Anthology

*Thanks to my husband Kevin for believing in me when I felt like I couldn't write another word.*

*Thank you, Ash, for the language advice.*

*Thank you to my writing group for their positive feedback when given tiny snippets to critique.*

*Thanks to my beta readers Ian, Donna, Claire and Zharel – you rock.*

*And finally, huge thanks to the talented Ian Bristow of Bristow Design for such a great cover.*

# Prologue

'De'been annuda one.'

'Who?'

'A pixie.'

'That makes two, yeah? Can we tell 'im now?'

'No, chil'. Is bes'we look afta we own.' Momma K, the ebony skinned, diminutive queen of the Fae, turned to face her wayward daughter, Jenni the sprite. Jenni was blonde haired and tall for a sprite, with a fierce attachment to her filthy red coat. The two fae couldn't be more different.

'But 'e could 'elp! Murder's murder and 'e wouldn't stop till 'e found 'im,' Jenni pleaded, her bare feet stamping in the grass. 'E's a good man and...'

Momma K cut her off with a dismissive flick of her wrist. 'De shapeshifta will be caught and called to trial fi him crimes. Me have a plan.'

'Yeah but 'ow many more will 'e kill before then? At least let me put an alert out on 'im?'

Momma K shook her head, making tiny charms tinkle in her silver dreadlocks, and glared fiercely at her daughter. 'We must guide him gently to de noose. Him will pay.' Looking at the darkening sky she lifted one hand, her fingers dancing in the dying light. 'Ya should return. Be ready fi ya'role when de time comes.'

'Yes, Momma K.' Jenni inclined her head in deference, and with a greasy popping sound, disappeared out of the fae grove.

# Chapter 1

Ned Spinks left The Noose and caught sight of his second-in-command loitering outside. His long brown coat swirled around his calves, dusting the tops of his battered old boots while he patted its pockets looking for his pipe. A power well and spell-casters belt hung unobtrusively about his waist and a small badge pinned to the lapel of his coat indicated his Chief Thief-Catcher status. Jenni wore a similar badge on her red coat. It was the only concession the thief-catchers made to a uniform.

'Ah, Jenni. There you are. Everything alright?' he asked.

'Yeah.' Jenni shoved her hands into her pockets. 'Sup?'

'There's been a murder. Possibly.'

'Why only possibly?'

'There is some trouble translating, which is why I was looking for you. Come on, we're going to the Big House.' Ned strode off, leaving Jenni to scramble after him. He towered over her; a dark, brooding figure next to her brighter but smellier, childlike appearance. In fact, if you ignored the tail sticking out of her coat and her hairy sprite ears, you might think father and daughter were out for a walk.

The Big House, as it was known locally, was the second largest dwelling in Roshaven and home to the distinguished Shillot family. Only the Emperor had more square footage. At dinner parties the Shillot's liked to jest that they might not be the biggest house in the city, but they were there first and surely that was more impressive, don't you agree? Ned had never been invited to one of those dinner parties and probably never would, so he was looking forward to having a poke around.

'Is one of the toffs dead?' asked Jenni.

'No, one of their brownies is. The others are proving difficult to understand. I know you'll have to report it to Momma K, being a fae murder, but first you can translate for me.'

'Yeah, 'course,' replied Jenni, her heart sinking. This made three. Three fae deaths - a nixie, a pixie and now a brownie.

The Big House had a tall, red-brick wall stretching for several metres either side of a pair of highly ornate metal gates which were currently closed. Ned pushed on the gates, but they remained unyielding. He was unsuccessfully looking for a doorbell of some kind when Jenni snapped her fingers and a squeal of resisting metal resulted in a human-shaped hole between the bars.

'I'm not paying for that, it's coming out of your wages,' Ned said as the two of them climbed through the gate.

Jenni snapped her fingers and the metal screeched back into place. Ned shook his head and began the long walk up the white stone drive. They passed immaculately kept flower beds and intricately pruned shrubbery before finally reaching the mansion. Row upon row of windows glittered in the sunlight and a fountain tinkled in the courtyard.

As they walked closer Jenni began to hear high-pitched chattering. Brownies didn't speak to humans very much but when they did, it was difficult to understand them due to their preferred frequency of communication. Sharp, shrill, squeaking. But from what she could make out, they were screeching, *'Murder!*

*Murder!'*

'You hear that, Jenni?'

'Yeah.'

Ned marched up to the front door of the Big House and was about to rap his knuckles on it, when it flung open.

'Thank the emperor - *may he live for ever and ever*! You will try not to make too much mess, won't you? I want it to be as painless as possible. For me. The whole thing has been such an ordeal. You know?' A tall, angular woman with shoulder length straight black hair clutched her hands to her chest and blinked expectantly.

'We'd like to speak with the brownies, please Ma'am.'

'Whatever for?'

'As part of our investigation. Into the murder.'

'Murder?' The thin lady looked behind her and then back at Ned and Jenni. 'So, you're not the exterminators?'

'No, we ain't!' snapped Jenni as she pushed past the woman and into the house.

'Thief-Catchers, Ma'am. At your service.' Ned smiled as the woman stepped backwards, letting him into the house.

It wasn't difficult to find the brownies, all they had to do was follow the noise until it got to ear-splitting level. Jenni wove her fingers in a complicated pattern and with a scattering of gold stars cast a silencer spell. It took the brownies a moment or two to realise that their yelling was now noiseless. As one, the group turned on Ned, gesturing wildly.

He fingered his spell-casting belt but knew he didn't have the power or skill to match, let alone undo Jenni's magic.

'Oi!' yelled Jenni, getting the brownie's attention. 'I

ain't giving you back your pipes 'til you cool it, right? You there,' she pointed to the tallest of the brownies. 'Oose in charge?'

The brownie scowled at Jenni before pointing to his left at the squat, fat one.

'Awright, I'm gonna give you your voice back.' Jenni swivelled slightly and pointed. 'But only youse, 'kay?' She flicked her fingers and, at once, a long stream of high-pitched profanity swept forwards.

'I say. This is all rather jolly, isn't it? Shall I ring for some tea?' There was slight desperation to Lady Shillot's voice as she did her best to smear manners over the unwanted guests in her drawing room. She didn't wait for an answer as she made her way across the room to pull the large rope dangling beside the mirror. Ned couldn't hear anything as she did it - but he never said no to a cuppa.

'Thank you, Ma'am.' He turned to face the chief brownie. 'Now, what happened?'

There was much squeaking.

'Jenni?'

'Wot? Oh right. Look, Boss, this'll probably go quicker if I spell youse.' And Jenni conjured some silver stars in Ned's face. They made him sneeze.

'Bless you! Would you like a hanky?' Lady Shillot looked on in fascination.

'No, thank you, Ma'am.' Ned tried again with the brownie. 'What happened here?'

'As I was trying to tell you fifty million times, he's killed Kevin! I don't know why that is so difficult for you to comprehend but there it is - dead as a gnorlax - and all we're getting is persecution for being loud! Kevin is dead. Where is the compassion? The sympathy? The cake?' The chief was so indignant that his jowls quivered.

'Cake? I can ring for some cake if you like, if it would help.' Lady Shillot hovered helpfully.

'If you wouldn't mind, Ma'am,' replied Ned. Then he did a double take. 'Do you speak Brownese?'

'Oh no. That's not one of my languages, I'm afraid. Daddy didn't think we should learn anything irregular.'

'So 'ow did you know 'e wanted cake?' asked Jenni.

'They always want cake, those things. Poor Cookie is in a dreadful state, always having to bake sweet. She never gets to do much savoury.'

The door to the drawing room opened and the butler appeared. Ned could tell he was the butler because he looked very disapprovingly at everything, including Lady Shillot.

'Ah, Jenkins. Could you bring us some tea and cake? There's a good chap.'

'As you wish, Ma'am.' The butler retreated silently. Ned wondered if they'd actually get any refreshments and if they did, how long it would take before they arrived.

'What are you going to do about it then?' A small voice demanded.

Ned tried to get back to the murder in hand. 'Tell me exactly what happened.'

'We had a new arrival. It's not unusual. Brownies come and brownies go. It's all part of cake-up. With there being so many bakers in the city, it's our duty to keep them on their toes and continue to check residencies for any new tasty slices. Why, only the other day Aggie made an adjustment to her cinnamon twist and claimed it was improved. She needs brownie approval to declare that, you know?'

Ned nodded in agreement. His waistline was all too

aware how great Aggie's cinnamon twists were.

'So, we had this new brownie - name of Arnold - and he wasn't that taken by the fruit cake we had. I thought to myself then he was unusual. Fruit cake is the centre of the universe, you know?' The chief waited for Ned to nod in agreement. He didn't. This was met with a disapproving stare and a harrumph.

'He asked a lot of questions, did Arnold.' The chief continued in a slightly miffed tone. 'Why this and why that. He spent time with everyone and was always looking closely at everything as if he was trying to take a picture with his mind or something.'

'How does that relate to the murder of Kevin?' asked Ned.

'Well, can you see Arnold here?' retorted the chief.

Ned shrugged helplessly.

'He's not. He disappeared shortly after we found Kevin's body inside the salad bowl! The salad bowl!'

The other brownies had been listening intently and at the mention of the salad bowl, they became very agitated.

'Brownies don't like salad, Boss - say it's devil food.'

'I'm quite partial to a seasonal leaf,' piped up Lady Shillot.

'I bet you are,' remarked Jenni.

The door opened and the butler returned with two trays, tea and small slices of cake on one and a mound of cake assortments on the other. The instant it was put down the brownies swarmed the second tray. Unsure of the etiquette here, Ned approached the tea cautiously. Jenkins poured and then held out a cup and saucer with as much disdain as a butler can summon. Ned mumbled a quiet thanks as the butler poured a cup for Jenni. She promptly tipped up the cup and slurped from her saucer loudly.

'S'awright that,' she burped. The butler flinched as she frisbeed him the china saucer, wiping the back of her mouth at the same time. He made the catch expertly, his face a slightly paler shade of disapproval than before.

The brownies slowed in their cake devouring and the chief shook himself free of crumbs.

'What are you going to do about Kevin, then?' he asked.

'I take it, he is no longer in the salad bowl?' asked Ned.

'Of course not! Why?'

'Would it be possible to see the body?'

There was much puffing of cheeks and pursing of lips.

'I suppose it would be alright. But they need their voices back and she's not coming.' The chief pointed at the rest of the brownies and then at Lady Shillot who was still sipping her tea.

Jenni rolled her eyes and clicked her fingers. Suddenly, there was a great deal of audible chittering among the brownies. She shushed them.

'Ma'am, we're going to go and see the victim now,' said Ned.

'How ghastly! Do you think there'll be any blood? Should I get changed? I want to create the right impression but, really, what does one wear to a murder scene?'

'Oh no, Ma'am. You need to stay here while we investigate. Official Thief-Catchers only.'

Lady Shillot's face fell but she quickly plastered her best fake smile on and pulled her shoulders back. 'Not to worry, one completely understands. Important business, of course. Will you be staying for supper?'

'No, thank you, Ma'am.' Ned faced the brownies and was relieved to see they were still waiting for him. 'After you.' He followed them out of the drawing room and down the corridor to a large tapestry hanging on the wall. The brownies started vanishing, one by one, as they walked through the tapestry. Ned frowned and bent down slightly to see what was happening. The bottom of the hanging was a little uneven and somewhat dog-eared. A section had rotted away, revealing a small door painted in the same colours as the tapestry to increase the camouflage. 'I'm not going to fit in there,' muttered Ned, trying unsuccessfully to channel some power from his well for a shrinking spell.

'Not to worry, Boss.' Jenni grinned and clapped her hands. She knew her boss struggled with spell-casting at times and was always happy to use her own magic for the both of them.

The door suddenly looked much more imposing. It was being held open by the chief who was no longer so squat but much more mountainous.

'Come on then, if you're coming.'

Ned made sure Jenni had shrunk with him, then they both walked through the opening into a warm tunnel, softly lit by glowbugs hanging on the wall. They followed the delicate scent of cinnamon and warm sugar, hints of vanilla and almond and the delicious aroma of baked confectionery until they reached an open cavern. The floor was covered in the crumbs of multiple devastated cakes.

'We must be under the kitchen,' mused Ned, looking around.

'Best place to be, don't know why people try to live anywhere else,' said the chief. 'This is where we found Kevin.' He pointed to a round wooden bowl, the sort of bowl that you would indeed use for salad. It was engraved with what could have been fat tomatoes.

'If you don't like salad, 'ow comes you 'ave a salad bowl?' asked Jenni.

'Kevin liked the shape. He said it cradled him beautifully at night and there was lots of space for cakage. He called it bowl liberation.' The chief blew his nose loudly.

Ned moved closer to have a look. There was nothing in the bowl, no fibres or handy murder weapons. 'And this is where you found him?'

'Yes.'

'At what time?'

'It was before first breakfast. Kevin is partial to a croissant, see. And you have to be quick to get 'em cos the big lady is a bit tight when it comes to morning pastries.'

'And there were no croissants?' asked Ned.

'No, it wasn't that. Derek had already done the run. Kevin never came to get his.'

'Do you always share breakfast?' Ned peered deeply into the bowl, trying to find some sort of clue. He would've attempted to open his fourth eye to find out what it saw but he had to be on top form to get it to work and right now he felt small.

The chief glared at him. 'We're not animals, you know!'

'No, no, of course not.' Ned looked at Jenni for some magical assistance.

'Er... I can do a time spell, Boss. See what 'appened or at least a 'pression of what 'appened.'

'Yes, please do.'

The brownies and Ned watched as Jenni cast her spell. Lots of little blue shapes ran around madly as she took a magical look back in time.

'Stop!' shouted Ned, pointing at the bowl. 'Looks like Kevin is going to sleep.'

They all watched in silence as nothing happened. Jenni scratched her armpit vigorously and was debating digging her ear wax out when a figure crept along the wall, towards the bowl. There was no one else around.

'Can we get a clear look at that face, Jenni?'

'See what I can do, Boss.' She waved her hands around in a complicated pattern and the blue shape became more detailed. It was definitely a brownie and he had a rather neat moustache.

'That's Arnold,' said the chief.

'That's unusual, isn't it? You don't normally go in for that sort of facial hair, do you?' Ned asked.

'We just thought it was because he was from out of town. You know, had some misplaced ideas of grandeur.'

The two figures merged, and it was difficult to see exactly what happened until Arnold left the salad bowl and Kevin lay unmoving, arms and legs spread out in unnatural positions.

'Is that how you found him?' asked Ned.

'Pretty much.'

'Ow comes you moved the body?' asked Jenni, collapsing her spell.

'It was putting the little ones off their cake. We've put him in cold storage.'

'Under the fridge?' guessed Ned.

The chief brownie nodded and led them over to a curtained off part of the cavern. 'This is where we store cream cakes, if they're not immediately eaten. Sometimes, the big lady has parties and she always over orders. Believe it or not, there is a limit to how much cream you can eat at one time.'

Jenni snorted in amusement.

The chief drew back the curtain and there lay Kevin. Arms and legs still splayed uncomfortably, eyes glazed over, his tongue sticking out of the corner of his mouth. He'd turned the colour of old cream and there was the faintest whiff of stale cake about him.

Ned took a good look at the body and noticed a silvery residue around Kevin's mouth. 'What's that?'

'Kevin's face,' replied the chief, frowning at Ned.

'No, that silvery stuff around his mouth.'

Jenni leaned in for a closer look but said nothing.

'Hmm, not sure,' replied the chief.

'Jenni? What do you think it is?' Ned asked but she shrugged and began inspecting her fingernails. Ned frowned but didn't press her. Maybe it was something she wanted to tell him away from the brownies. He spoke instead to the chief. 'And there's been no sign of Arnold since?'

'No. He's gone. His bag's gone. Even his emergency cake allowance has gone - and he had some of the best icing we've had for ages.'

'And Kevin didn't have any enemies among your clan?'

'No. He shared. That's the mark of a great brownie.' The chief turned away to take a speck of something out of his eye.

'Do we have a clear image of the murderer's face, Jenni?' asked Ned.

'Yeah, spose.'

'Alright then, we'll take the image back to HQ and get some wanted posters drawn up.' Ned turned to the chief. 'We'll make some enquiries and begin a search for Arnold. A brownie by himself won't be too difficult to find. I'll let you know as soon as we learn anything.' He shook hands solemnly with the chief and motioned for Jenni to follow him out of the brownie cavern. As they emerged from the tapestry, she regrew them, which gave Ned sudden head rush.

Lady Shillot bustled over. 'Well? Are they going to stop all this clamouring? I've got a cocktail party tonight and my guests will be really dismayed if they have to listen to that racket.'

'We have concluded our investigation, for the time being. We may need to return with further questions. If I were you, I'd make sure you have plenty of cake on hand for the funeral and for the grieving process,' said Ned.

'Yes, of course. One must do what one can.' She blinked at them hopefully. 'If that's all?'

'Very good, Ma'am.' Ned raised two fingers to his head and tipped them toward her before ushering Jenni out of the house.

'I'd say that was a straightforward whodunnit, eh, Jenni?'

'Mmm.'

'All we have to do is find this Arnold chappie - shouldn't be too difficult. I suspect the fact that he's run away means the whole thing was an accident. It's not like brownies are known for their murderous tendencies, is it?'

'Pends on the cake, I guess.'

'Are you alright, Jenni? You seem a bit...'

'Yeah.' Jenni hawked and spat. 'Look, Boss. I gotta go see Momma K 'bout summik.'

'Right. Can you report the brownie death to her as well then, please? Seeing as it's a fae murder, she needs to know.'

'Yep. Laters.' And Jenni popped out of sight, leaving

her unique scent behind.

# Chapter 2

Oblivious to the sweet scent that wafted invitingly, Jenni hurried past the giant strawberries; for once not even thinking about stealing one for later. She easily found Momma K. She was sat on her favourite toadstool, meditating. The sky above was a calm milky blue.

'What ya got to tell me?' asked Momma K, one eyebrow raised.

'We've 'ad a novver one.'

'Who was it dis time?'

'A brownie. Called Kevin. Poor fing was murdered inna salad bowl.'

Momma K scowled and thunder clouds gathered. No one deserved to be murdered in a salad bowl. 'Dis shapeshifta is working him way through us. Me have to stop him.'

'Are you gonna ask for 'elp now?'

Momma K didn't reply but the sky rumbled so Jenni tried a different approach.

'I ain't 'appy about popping back and forth 'ere like a yoyo. Do you 'ave to see me every time summik 'appens?'

'I prefer to talk to ya in person. Keep ya honest about what ya be doin' and who ya loyalty belong.'

'Yeah, but...'

Momma K tsked at her daughter and closed her eyes, giving the impression she had returned to her meditation. The crackle of lightning through the stormy sky suggested otherwise.

Jenni huffed but knew she couldn't change Momma

K's mind. Jenni might be her daughter and possible heir to the fae kingdom, but Momma K had no intention of stepping down anytime soon. They clashed on many things, including Jenni's preference to work as a thief-catcher. *Probably why she were so against using Ned to 'elp catch the shifter*, thought Jenni. But maybe she could apprehend the murderer by herself, without any help from Momma K or Ned. What she needed to do was open a file. If only she'd paid attention at work when it was time to do the paperwork.

Ned wandered back to The Noose. It was a delightful little hostelry that perched jauntily on the edge of the aptly named Black Narrows and also acted as headquarters for the Thief-Catchers in the rooms upstairs. And if by delightful you mean grime encrusted walls, floors and ceiling; a barman who'd sooner shoot you than serve you; and a clientele that lacked a certain respectability; then yes, The Noose was extremely delightful.

Ned had the uncomfortable feeling that someone was watching him and was hoping to catch sight of them before he reached the pub. The itching between his shoulder blades was constant yet whenever he turned around, he saw nothing. With regret he tried to push the feeling to the back of his mind and focus on the task ahead. He needed to get in the office and open a file on the murder of Kevin, but he also needed Jenni's magic. He'd forgotten to get the picture from the spell she cast. He remembered there was a moustache but in order to get some wanted posters printed, he needed that image. Perhaps *The Daily Blag* would run a piece for him.

Reg, the taciturn barman at The Noose, was standing outside the pub. This was not a good sign. Reg never left the bar, ever. Ned approached him cautiously. He could hear a great deal of hooting and whistling from inside, but it wasn't Thursday. Yvette von Strunkle wasn't due to perform so Ned wondered what on earth was exciting the usually morose patrons.

'Reg.'

'Ned.'

There was a pause.

'Nice day,' said Ned, hoping to get away with a little small talk.

'Hmm.'

'Right, well, I'll head up if there's nothing else.'

'There's nixies in the pub.'

'What?' Ned was surprised. The river sprites very rarely left the River Whine, not even to visit Piss Eyed Nellie in her lake. The fact that several of them had risked coming on land meant there must be a huge problem. And it explained why Reg had spoken more than two words. Typically, he didn't hold with conversation of any kind unless it was an emergency situation and even then Reg felt that monosyllables worked just fine. 'I'll sort it out.'

'They're naked.'

Ned sighed. He hoped there weren't too many patrons inside. He patted Reg's shoulder as he went past and walked into the heaving pub. No one was crowded around the bar, demanding drinks. Which was a good thing, considering the barman was outside, having a moment. Instead, the focus of the room was at the back, where the rickety stairs that led up to Ned's offices could be found. There were three naked women standing on the stairs. To their credit, they were doing a great job of ignoring the leering mass of mankind gathered below them. And the fact they were completely transparent did nothing to lessen their womanly bareness.

'Pardon me. Excuse me. Sorry.' Ned pushed his way through the throng, to the bottom of the stairs, and then wished he hadn't. He craned his neck as far back as he could to avert his eyes.

'Ladies, may I help?'

'We've come to see Jenni.'

'Ah. She's not here at the moment. But I'm expecting her back soon. Would you like to wait upstairs?' Ned really hoped they did.

The nixies nodded in harmony and glided up the stairwell. Ned followed them, making sure he took the opportunity to thoroughly inspect his boots. Once he'd climbed up a few stairs, he was able to catch the attention of Mortar, the troll bouncer for The Noose.

'Can you guard the bottom of the stairs?' Ned shouted. 'Unless it's thief-catcher business, no one comes up, alright?'

'No problem.' Mortar cracked his knuckles loudly and the disappointed patrons grumbled as they headed en masse to the bar. Reg had recovered and was back in his customary place, dirty tea towel over one shoulder.

Ned left them to it, confident that Mortar could deal with any trouble. He took a deep breath as he climbed the rest of the stairs and entered his office, preparing himself to look anywhere but at naked women. He needn't have worried. The three nixies had turned their forms opaque in the places where a dress would fall. Sparks, his firefly thief-catcher, was flitting about, flashing his tail but that was nothing unusual. Ned's latest recruit, Joe, was hovering by the filing cabinet and blushing furiously. This too was nothing new. He was a young lad with an overactive Adam's apple and rather large ears.

'Hi, Boss. I told them this might work better?' It was Willow, the wood-nymph thief-catcher, who knew all about the difficulties in attracting too much human attention. It was something she dealt with on a regular basis and was the reason why Ned wore a bracelet of her hair – to guard against her magical attractiveness.

'Excellent, good thinking, Willow. Ladies, can I get you anything while you wait?'

The three nixies sloshed a little as they conferred briefly. 'Maybe you can help us? Do you have an update on who killed Brook?'

Ned looked at them blankly.

'Our sister. She was murdered eleven days ago. We told Momma K and Jenni, but we haven't heard anything since.'

'Oh right, yes. Sorry, we've had a lot of cases recently,' Ned said, thinking fast.

Sitting idly by the window, Willow bloomed in surprise. They'd hardly had anything lately.

'Remind me of the details, if you don't mind, er... what's your name?'

'I'm Babble,' one of the nixies said, stepping forward. 'Our sister, Brook, was found dead. She was evaporated.'

Willow turned a sickly green.

'Forgive me for being insensitive, but how do you know?' asked Ned.

'When a nixie is killed, the magical properties holding their fluids together dissipates and the liquid evaporates. It leaves behind a shape - the favourite form of that particular nixie, so we can honour them and perform their last rites.'

'What form did Brook leave behind?'

'A water horse. But she was found on gravel! A nixie

would never go to gravel to die. And she was young, strong. Her magics had only recently manifested. And there was...' Babble put a watery hand to her mouth. 'There was some kind of silvery residue.'

'Have you had a new nixie visit you recently?' asked Ned.

'Why, yes. How did you know?'

'Did he have a moustache?'

'Yes. We all thought it was very strange. Nixies don't have hair but he was from out of river and they do strange things in the north, so we just thought it was one of their oddities. He asked lots of questions and spent an awful lot of time watching Brook.'

'What was his name?'

'Armand.'

*Close enough,* thought Ned. 'I need to come out, view the crime scene - if that's possible?' he asked.

'Jenni has already been, she's already taken statements. She asked for privacy when she cast the time spell, but she told us she had some leads. We've come for an update. Armand has completely disappeared. We think he might have had something to do with it.'

'I think you may be right,' replied Ned.

Jenni popped into the room, making Joe jump.

'Jenni!' The three nixies chorused loudly in relief.

'Snails!'

Ned said nothing, waiting for an explanation.

'We've come for an update,' said Babble hopefully.

'Er...' Jenni glanced at Ned. 'See, fing is... wot it is right... er...'

Ned stepped in. 'As I was saying ladies, we needed to investigate the scene. And now that Jenni has done that, we will look at all the evidence and start following up leads. It's a busy time for us, as you can imagine, but we will be in touch soon. You have my word on that.'

The nixies didn't look too impressed but allowed themselves to be ushered out of the office by a very deferential Willow. They were cousins of a sort, and it's always sad to hear of a death in the family.

After the nixies had left, Ned rounded on Jenni. 'You've got some serious explaining to do but first, I need the picture of Arnold, the brownie, from your time spell this morning. Then, once you've done that, you'd better give me the details of this nixie murder.'

'But Boss, this is fae stuff. You ain't got to get involved. I got this.'

'Not anymore you don't. I can't ignore a crime on my doorstep, and you didn't even know about the brownies, did you?'

Jenni shook her head slowly. 'Momma K ain't gonna like it.'

'I don't care. This is what we do. I'm not having Roshaven citizens thinking we can't protect them. So, give me those pictures, please.'

Jenni huffed and puffed but did as she was asked and there was a good ten minutes of silence as Ned opened two case files, Sparks hovering helpfully over his shoulder. Ned peered closely at the two images but the only linking factor was the facial hair. Arnold, the brownie, looked like a brownie and Armand, the nixie, looked like a nixie. The only similarity was the name. Could they be adopted brothers, perhaps?

Jenni watched her boss but said nothing. If he came to the shapeshifter conclusion on his own, then fine. Otherwise, this was still a fae case and she was going to crack it. She wasn't going to tell Momma K that Ned knew some of the other murder details either, not yet anyway.

'Wot's next then, Boss?'

'We start canvassing the area.'

Willow coughed and shook her leaves nervously. 'Um, Boss? Isn't this fae territory? Shouldn't we leave it to Momma K to sort out? We don't want to step on any roots.'

'No, Willow. I feel very strongly about this. A crime has been committed – two crimes. If we can't catch a murderer, then we shouldn't be thief-catchers.'

'I thought we only caught thieves,' ventured Joe, earning himself a glare from Ned which set his Adam's apple off.

'Theft of life is a crime as much as theft of an item. We are thief-catchers. We will investigate the crime and we will uphold the law. Any more ridiculous questions?'

Joe shook his head so fast it looked like it might fall off, Willow pressed her lips together but said nothing, and Jenni remained quiet as well.

'Everyone knows what they're looking for?' asked Ned.

'Looking for a tache, right?' replied Jenni.

'A brownie and a nixie, both with a particularly neat moustache,' corrected Ned.

'Yeah, that's wot I meant.'

Ned frowned. Something wasn't quite right about any of this, in particular, Jenni's reaction. 'Willow, Sparks, you take the public green spaces. Speak to the foliage and the bugs, see what you can unearth. Jenni, you take the west side of town, get their story. I'll do the east side. Speak to as many magical denominations as you can.'

'Cept for the pixies,' said Jenni.

'Why can't we speak to the pixies?' asked Willow.

'Cos. You know what they're like. Pack o' liars, the

lot of 'em. Best if I deal wiv the pixies.'

Willow shrugged and collected her paperwork with pictures of Arnold and Armand. 'Don't forget, I have to finish at four today, Boss. I've got my fertilisation treatment booked; things are a little dull.' She ran her hand over her wooden body in a way that set Ned's heart thumping despite his protection charm. Poor Joe had to sit down and put his head in his hands. There was a great deal of heavy breathing.

'Yes, good. No problem. Good luck, Willow. And Sparks.'

'Thanks, Boss,' said Willow cheerfully as Sparks zipped around her trunk and they both left the office.

'Yeah, I'll catch you laters, Boss.' Jenni popped out of the office before Ned could reply, leaving him and his racing heart to deal with Joe.

'Joe?'

There was no answer.

'JOE!'

'Yes, Boss?'

'I want you to stay here - man the office.' Ned looked around at the various tottering piles of paper. He waved a hand at a particularly large pile. 'Maybe do a bit of filing or something.'

'Yes, Boss.'

Satisfied that even Joe couldn't mess that up, Ned set off on his own investigation. Somehow there was a connection between these two moustached fae and he would get to the bottom of it.

# Chapter 3

Ned didn't even get to the bottom of the stairs. Another woman was waiting for him on the stairwell, armed with pen and paper. It was Mariah Neeps, reporter and owner of *The Daily Blag*.

'Spinks.'

'Neeps.'

'Somewhere to be?'

'Wherever there's crime.'

'Oh, I like that. Mind if I quote you?' asked Neeps.

'Do I have a choice?'

Neeps grinned but didn't reply.

'Can I help you with something?' Ned didn't really want Neeps upstairs alone with Joe. The lad wasn't exactly the brightest star in the sky, and he didn't need another scathing story on the inefficiency of Thief-Catchers. It wasn't her fault that Willow had been unable to catch Devious Dave. He'd slathered himself in weed killer. His name was Devious Dave for a reason. And it wasn't Ned's fault that Neeps just happened to hear about the story of a thief-catcher failing to catch a thief.

'I wanted your take on the fae murders - for an article I'm writing.' Neeps smiled winningly.

'Have you cleared it with Momma K?' asked Ned. The fae queen could be touchy at having her realm and inhabitants discussed.

'Do I need to?'

'That's your mushroom ring, I guess.' Ned sighed. He had been thinking of telling Neeps what he knew, getting the details out. It might help with his investigation. 'Let's walk and talk,' he suggested, gesturing for Neeps to go back down the stairs.

'If you're sure you can keep up,' she replied.

Ned shook his head, smiling as he followed Neeps out of The Noose. At least his relationship with the press was civil. It was more than could be said for the various city guilds' relationship with the press. None of them were on speaking terms with the paper which suited Neeps just fine. It meant she could print whatever she liked about them.

As they strolled away from the Black Narrows, Ned veered east so he was at least walking in the right direction for his canvassing.

'Why don't you start by telling me what you know?' he asked her.

'I heard about a pixie and a gingerbread man this week. Last week it was a nixie and a harpy.'

Ned winced at that. The gingerbread people were nearly extinct. The spell that originally created them had been lost in an oven fire. The gingerbread people blamed the shortbread fingers, but they swore blind they'd had nothing to do with. At least they would've if they had eyes or mouths. Magically enhanced biscuitry was not Ned's favourite denizen of Roshaven.

'Any facts you can confirm?' asked Neeps.

'The nixies lost a sister; Brook. She was evaporated by the looks of things. I've also had a brownie murder reported this morning; Kevin was found in a salad bowl. Both murders contain a moustache.'

'A moustache? What did it do? Suffocate them to death?' Neeps tried not to laugh.

'I mean, both suspects had one. You can put that in your report. Anyone seen behaving suspiciously, with a particularly neat moustache, should be reported.'

'I can't do that. You'll end up with hundreds of dead ends.'

'At least we'd have some leads,' muttered Ned. He felt sure Jenni knew about the pixies. That would have been why she was so insistent that no one went to see them. If she already knew about the harpy and the gingerbread man as well, then Momma K must be forcing her to keep secrets. It wasn't like Jenni to lie. Stink to high heaven and steal the occasional baked good, yes. But not lie.

'So, no leads. Facial hair was prominent in both crimes. Anything else?' asked Neeps.

'You seem to know more than me. What have you got?'

Neeps flipped back in her notepad and began reading her notes aloud. 'Pixies reported a murder. They had a visitor - Aranis or something similar – who had a moustache. Unusual for pixies but they said he was from out of town, so they figured that was the reason.' She glanced up at Ned briefly before carrying on. 'The harpies reported a death, in the water - very uncharacteristic, as you know they don't bathe. No mention of facial hair, but they closed ranks and refused to answer when I asked about any new visitors lately. So, could be they're hiding something.'

Ned nodded and added a visit to the harpies to his mental list. He'd take Jenni with him. The harpies gave him the collywobbles. It was the teeth and the claws and the smell. Plus, the fact they ate human flesh, raw. He shivered.

'And then... ah, here we are. The gingerbread people. They lost one of their elders. He already had a crumbly leg and had lost his buttons. They'd been trying to protect him from moisture, keeping him away from rivers and foxes, that sort of thing. But then... huh.'

'What? They had a visitor?'

'Yeah... a new gingerbread man. Highly iced. With a particularly neat moustache.' Neeps stared at Ned. 'Why do all the suspects have the same facial hair? It can't be the same person, can it?'

Ned shrugged and scratched his head. He didn't see how it could be, but he also couldn't see how it wasn't. Although - Jenni's reluctance to involve him and the fact that all the victims were fae probably meant the killer was some kind of fae as well. But what?

'Well, thanks for this,' said Neeps, putting her pen and paper away in her bag. 'I'll run an information request in the paper with the whole moustache thing, but I don't know how helpful it will be.'

'Cheers. I appreciate it.'

'Where are you headed now?' she asked.

'Well, I was going to canvas the east side of Roshaven with the pictures we got from the nixie and brownie crime scenes, but now I'm wondering if there is any point,' replied Ned.

'I'll take a couple. I can put them with the info request in the paper.' Neeps held out her hand for the pictures. 'You never know; the specific facial hair might remind some people of a shifty person they've seen lately. That's what you want, isn't it?'

Ned nodded and handed over the images. He said goodbye to Neeps and strode off to the eastern part of the city. There was a notice board in the public square where he could put the 'Information Wanted' posters he'd printed. Then, Queen Ann might see him, always worth getting the beggar network on your own side. He checked his pockets, but there wasn't much in there apart from one gold coin he'd been saving for new boots. It should be a big enough payment for the beggar network.

Intent on the task ahead, Ned didn't notice the fae eyes watching him travel through the city. Momma K didn't trust Jenni to keep Ned out of the murder investigations and wanted to know how much she was involving him. Fae justice tended to be bloodier than Roshaven justice and wasn't officially approved by the emperor.

# Chapter 4

Momma K cut the connection with her fae spy and opened her inky black eyes to gaze at Jenni who had just arrived. 'Ummhmm, why ya here?' she demanded. Her realm's sky was rose petal pink with hints of exasperated purple, and it smelled of fried onions.

'The nixies came to The Noose. They want answers,' replied Jenni, wrinkling her nose.

'If ya doin' ya job propa, dey would already 'ave dem.'

'That ain't fair!' protested Jenni.

'Me doh' see a shapeshifta in me prison.'

'Yeah, well, Ned knows all about it now anyways.'

'Me see.' Momma K flexed her wings.

'You spying on me?'

Momma K fluttered upwards, her petite body framed by two gloriously patterned silver and black slender wings. Jenni was forced to tip her head back in order to keep looking at the fae.

'Ya dare question? Me trying to catch a murdera.'

Jenni looked away then spat on the path in annoyance. 'Whatever. Least I'm doing my job.'

'Tsk. Chil' ya fae first, catcha second. Dis is where ya focus should be. Here, in me kingdom.'

'I ain't 'aving this fight again. Give us a few days. Lemme fill Ned in wiv it all. We'll find 'im.'

Momma K floated down to the ground, landing next to her daughter and gracefully folded her wings away. 'I may not have much time, daughter. A reckoning a coming.'

'Whaddayamean?'

'Pixie, nixie, brownie, harpy and gingerbread man are too many fae deaths to ignore. And dis is not all. Me know of a golem too.'

Jenni whistled in surprise. 'Ned'll wanna know the details.'

Momma K glared at her daughter for a moment then snapped her fingers. 'Here is what me have. But doh' rely on ya human to solve dis.'

A file appeared and Jenni snatched it out of the air. She flicked through quickly. 'I fawt you didn't agree wiv paper.'

'Me doh', dis is for ya catchas. Me hear dey can't do anyting wi'out it.'

Jenni muttered under her breath but was careful not to grumble too loudly. The last thing she wanted was an actual argument with her queen. She definitely didn't want to argue with her mum. 'I can tell 'im it's a shapeshifter now, right?'

'No.'

'Why not?'

Momma K sniffed as she flew back to her toadstool. 'Me doh' want news of dis shifter in de city. Dere are nefarious factions who will try to use him for dere own gains. It best if we keep dis to ahselves.'

'Do you not fink they'll figure it out? It's kinda obvs.'

Momma K smiled. 'Ya be amazed what humans can ignore, chil'.' Then with a more serious face, she delivered her final words on the matter. 'Ya will no tell Spinks and ya will find de shifta first. Me no relying on a human to catch a fae. Use de resources ya tink are important and hurry. We do no have long.' She dismissed Jenni with a flick of her fingers and closed her eyes.

Jenni popped out of the fae realm grumbling to herself.

'Ow am I ever gonna find a bloody shifter if I can't tell anyone I'm looking for a bloody shifter? Stoopid bloody rules. Stoopid fae. Stoopid murders.' She sniffed the air and orientated herself. Ned was with the beggars, or he would be by the time she found him. She headed off to the far east side of Roshaven, where Queen Ann held her court.

Jenni beat Ned there by a few minutes. She was lounging against a wall, soaking up some sunshine when he strolled around the corner.

'Ah, Jenni. You're back.' He paused. 'Did you even go to the west side of town?'

Jenni scuffed her foot on the floor. Ned sighed.

'What did Momma K say?'

'Er... she ain't too 'appy but that ain't nuffink new.'

'She told you not to tell me anything, didn't she?'

'Not 'zactly. She gave you this.' Jenni handed Ned the paperwork file.

He flipped it open and skimmed the information inside, it wasn't much. Just the bare facts about the fae murders. At least he didn't have to canvas the city now. It looked like he had all the information he needed.

'She didn't tell you about my fae shadow, did she?' Ned shifted his head to the left slightly. He'd finally noticed he had a tail. Jenni glanced in that direction and saw a pair of eyes glowing faintly in the gloom.

'Nah.'

Ned leaned on the wall next to Jenni and took out his pipe. He took his time filling the bowl with tobacco and getting it to light. He puffed away in silence.

'You got 'em all now though, yeah?' Jenni asked eventually.

'Pixie, nixie, brownie, harpy and gingerbread man.'

'Anna golem.' Jenni flicked a pebble in the direction of the glowing eyes. With a little magical assist, it flew way further then it should've and there was a gasp when it hit its mark. The glowing eyes made a hasty retreat.

'You know she'll probably send someone else, right?' commented Ned.

'Yeah, I know.' Jenni dug her toe into a crevice between two cobbles. 'Sorry Boss.'

Ned knocked the ashes out of his pipe on the wall and put it back in its pouch. 'Do you know who the murderer is?'

Jenni sighed heavily. 'Yeah.'

'Are you going to tell me?'

'Can't.'

'Do you know where he is?'

'Nah.'

'Do you know how to find him?'

Jenni wouldn't meet Ned's gaze and shook her head mutely.

'Will you at least make sure I don't go off in completely the wrong direction?'

'Course.'

'Alright then. Let's go speak to the queen.'

They entered Queen Ann's court with Jenni occupying her usual defensive position; behind Ned, on his right-hand side. There were no distinguishing features that they had arrived at the beggar court per se, it was the change in ripeness that alerted them to having arrived in the right place. That and the various beggars loitering in the area, rattling their begging bowls. It was a dead giveaway.

A large pile of rags had been discarded against one wall. Flies swarmed thickly. One might think it was a heap of discarded rubbish. One would be wrong. A slender finger topped with a long, dirty nail curled over and beckoned them. At least Ned thought it was beckoning them. He looked around hastily, but there was no one else nearby.

'Er... your majesty?' he asked tentatively.

The heap shuddered and a head emerged from the pile. The accompanying smell was enough to stagger Ned backwards a few paces. Even Jenni whistled at the stench. It was impressive. It had layers. You could chew it.

'Please, approach the crown.' The voice was dusky and rich. Not what you would expect from the exterior rags. Rumour had it that Queen Ann was a bored daughter of the emperor - *may he live for ever and ever -* who had decided she could have more fun out of the palace than in it.

Ned took one cautious step forward. He didn't want to soak up too much smell and have it accompanying him for the rest of the day.

'What can one do for you, catcher?'

'We're looking for a suspicious moustache.'

There was a throaty laugh. 'Just a moustache? Or perhaps one attached to a murderous individual?'

'So, you know?' Despite himself, Ned leaned forward. It was a mistake. His eyes began to water, and he had to put a hand to his nose.

'One can tell you are overcome in the presence of royalty.' Two green eyes stared at Ned intently. 'Come into ones chambers, where we can talk more comfortably.'

The heap shuffled sideways into a concealed entrance that led into a building. Abruptly, the heap was discarded and a slender young woman wearing a pale blue dress stepped out of the rags and shook herself. She stepped through an empty floor length mirror frame and emerged with the faintest hint of a pleasant floral perfume.

'One of yours?' Ned asked Jenni.

She nodded proudly.

Ned was impressed, the queen now smelled as he imagined actual royalty would. 'Your Majesty, please, tell me what you know about the recent fae murders.'

Queen Ann sat down in a large, floral-patterned armchair and indicated two nearby stools. Jenni sat easily, but the stool was a little too close to the floor for Ned to sit down with ease. He got there eventually with his knees bent up by his ears.

'As you know, one has a small network of eyes and ears in Roshaven.'

Jenni snorted and the queen glared at her.

'Ahem. Our little network has noticed the same moustache appearing on different creatures of fae. What you've got is...'

Jenni interrupted. 'Moostaches are in this season. Was finking of growing one meself. It ain't no kind of evidence for nuffink.'

The queen ignored Jenni entirely and focused all her attention on Ned. 'What you've got is a cult.'

'A cult?'

'Isn't it obvious? They all have a distinguishing mark, and they are scattered across denizens who don't normally fraternise. Someone is bringing fae together. Momma K ought to be worried.'

'Hmm, I suppose it's a possibility. But what's their motivation?' Ned was at a loss. 'How does killing random members of different fae communities affect Momma K?'

'It makes her look weak,' replied Queen Ann. 'And weakness in a monarch encourages factions to strike. You may remember the rebellion last spring when attention was not paid to the begging device used. A weakness on my part, and the start of a new idea.'

'Was that when the beggars started using signs instead of bowls?' asked Ned.

'It showed intelligence. And that, my friend, does a beggar no favours at all. One was quick to put a stop to that.'

'What do you think, Jenni?' asked Ned. 'Could that be the reason? I always thought Momma K was born to the fae throne by right and couldn't be challenged.'

'Yeah, well, fae's fickle ain't they. But mebbe, mebbe. Could be a cult.'

Ned narrowed his eyes at her. She didn't seem overly convinced, but he didn't want to get into it here. 'Thank you for your help, Your Majesty.' He dipped his head at the queen of beggars.

'No trouble at all.' A begging bowl appeared out of nowhere. It was silver and inlaid with precious gems. 'A small token of your appreciation, perhaps?'

Ned felt in his pocket for his single gold coin, but before he had the chance to draw it out, Jenni had filled the bowl. He stammered his thanks again and hurried to catch her up as she left the lair.

'That was a lot of gold, Jenni.'

'Yeah. Don't worry. It's chocolate coins,' she said with a snigger.

'Jenni!'

'Wot? She ain't paid me for that mirror. Call it evens.'

'It's not a good idea to upset the beggar community though, we really want them on our side.'

'Don't worry. They've gotta come recharge their glamours next week, and they get all that for free anyways.'

They walked along in silence for a while.

'It's not a cult, is it?' Ned asked finally.

'Nah.'

'But the moustache is important.'

'Yeah.'

'Maybe I should go talk to Momma K.'

'Wot for?'

'To ask her to let me help solve this case.'

'She ain't gonna let you, Boss.'

'I'm not going to stop investigating the murders.'

Jenni looked up and down the road, choosing to ignore the last statement. 'We going back to HQ?'

'Yes, we need to see what Willow and Sparks came up with and then get some interviews set up for this afternoon, if possible. Get some fae coming to us for a change.'

'They won't just come to you.'

'They might, if they're properly motivated.'

'Wot you finking, Boss?'

'You'll see.'

# Chapter 5

'Sparks?' Ned called out the firefly's name as he pushed open the office door and slung his coat on the hook, balancing the lunchtime pizza boxes from Gariboldi's in his other hand. 'I need you to send out some wanted messages.' There was no space on the table due to the tremendous amounts of paperwork waiting to be filed so Ned put the pizza boxes on the floor. He flipped open a lid, snagging a slice. The aroma of savoury yumminess filled the office while Sparks shone to attention. He wasn't that keen on pizza and had come back to the office before Willow to get a shot of nectar.

'Er, Boss? I don't fink this is a good idea,' said Jenni with her mouth full as she helped Sparks get into his messenger harness. He could carry four small messages in the tubes attached to the delicate leather contraption that now sat around his body. Jenni was also carefully watching Joe as he helped himself to a slice of pizza. She had her eye on the slightly burnt one and wasn't above fighting for it.

'Well, most of what I do on a daily basis probably isn't a good idea, Jenni. If nothing else, this will bring them to our door.' He walked towards his desk, which was working as scaffolding for his piles of paperwork, in order to clear a space but decided that was another day's problem and veered off to one side instead. He moved the foot and a half of paperwork off a nearby chair, placing it on the floor, then balanced the new case paperwork on his knees as he sat on the chair he'd unearthed. He looked around as the office door opened and Willow returned. 'How did it go?' he asked, through a bite of pizza.

'Bug pheromone had nothing to say and word on the grapevine is that this murderer is very good at getting in and out of places without being seen. I did ask about the moustache, but neither plants or insects really understand facial hair.' She shook her own leafy tresses. 'Sorry they weren't more helpful.'

'I appreciate the effort, Willow. I ran into Neeps and got some more intel, then Momma K gave us her murder file. We'll be doing some interviews here now. Can you sort out some more chairs? And you'd better go down and warn Reg.' Ned ate the rest of his pizza slice and grabbed a spare bit of parchment. After wiping his greasy hands on his trousers, he tore the paper into four and wrote wanted in big letters on each piece. 'Jenni? Who is the top pixie?'

'Sugar Puff the fird.'

'And the harpies?'

'Agatha. But Boss, honestly, this ain't a good idea.'

Ned nodded but didn't stop what he was doing. He wrote down *Gingerpeople* on the third summons and *The Golems* on the final one, then rolled them up into small cylinders and popped them into the messenger tubes.

'Sparks, take these to the heads of each group, please. The gingerbread people will probably send Man and the golem will send whoever the next number is. But make sure they know they are wanted for questioning in the murder of their fellow fae. They're people of interest, linked to the case, that sort of thing.'

'You don't think the gingerbread people killed one of their own, do you?' asked Willow, in the middle of growing chair legs.

'No but doing this should bring the relevant fae

leaders to us so we don't spend the afternoon running around Roshaven looking for them. Off you go Sparks.'

The firefly buzzed once and flitted toward the window, intent on his mission. It was unfortunate that the window happened to be closed. The bug bounced off the pane with a loud tink. Willow rushed over to check he was alright while Ned opened the window. The firefly shook his glow a couple of times before wobbling back into flight.

'Are you good?' Ned asked.

The firefly zipped and threw a salute. No one saw it, but it made Sparks feel better as he flew out of the window.

Ned surveyed the room. One half was taken up by his desk cunningly disguised as towering pillars of paperwork, but the rest of the room was relatively clear, if you didn't count the neat piles of folders that were stacked along the edges of the room. He unearthed another chair from the most stable paperwork pile, making sure it was fully supported by the other columns adjacent to it. With the chair he'd just used and a third that Willow made, all they needed now was another table to complete the appearance of a professional interview room.

'Jenni, can you go down and ask Reg for the fold out table, please? He doesn't need it until next Tuesday. Oh, and warn him who's coming, will you?'

Willow rustled. 'I thought you wanted me to do that?'

'Yes, sorry. As long as someone does it.'

The door banged as Jenni did as she was asked, taking the burnt pizza slice with her. Willow went back to her chair, adding in extra scrollwork. Joe ventured forward for his third slice. Ned felt the first flicker of concern. Maybe this wasn't such a great idea. He was contemplating going to help Jenni with the table when, through the conveniently open window, the leader of the harpies, Agatha, arrived in a swirl of maddened feathers and rusty blood. Her talons scraped across the floor as her wings beat furiously, filling the room with her fetid stench. Joe cowered in his corner.

'How dare you accuse me of murdering my kin?' she screeched.

Ned valiantly stood his ground and hoped his wobbly knees weren't noticeable. 'Glad I got your attention. I have some questions about the murder of...' He paused to look down at his file then continued in a softer tone. 'My apologies, I don't know the victim's name.'

Agatha blinked, not expecting Ned's conciliatory tone. 'Her name was Brigitta. And you are not worthy of saying it. Maggot.'

'Right, lovely. If you wouldn't mind?' Ned calmly pointed to the beautiful chair Willow had grown and carefully walked past the harpy to take his seat opposite, wishing vehemently that a table was between them. He sat there with a pen and paper and tried to smile, heart thudding in his chest, sure the harpy could smell his fear.

'I have already reported the crime to Momma K.' Agatha stretched out her rust-coloured wings, momentarily making the room darker as she blocked out the light from the window. 'Brigitta was killed. What more could you possibly need to know?'

'Have you had any new members to your, er, murder, lately?' asked Ned, trying not to get distracted at the name for a collection of harpies.

Agatha frowned. 'Yes, we did. But she was a scrawny, blithering idiot who asked too many questions and suffered some kind of facial furring. We sent her away.'

'Facial furring, you say?' Ned frowned. That didn't fit with his male moustache theory. But then, he supposed women could have moustaches. He'd certainly seen them on female members of the Roshaven community. Granted, they were mostly dwarves. He made a note and risked another question. 'Did the idiot leave before or after Brigitta was murdered?'

The harpy sat with a thump. The chair creaked noisily. 'Before.'

'And it left no trace behind?'

The harpy shook her head then narrowed her eyes at Ned. 'You think this weakling overcame Brigitta? In a fight, she would never have won.'

'Murderers don't tend to fight fair,' he observed. 'One more question, if I may?'

Agatha paused then nodded curtly.

'Was there any silvery residue at the scene of the murder?'

'It's hard to say. She was murdered in water of all things and scavengers got to her body first. We had to search for parts before we could cook her funeral feast.'

Ned swallowed. He hoped that didn't mean what he thought it meant.

'She was delicious.'

It absolutely meant what he thought it meant.

'Okay, then. Thank you very much for coming in. You are no longer wanted in connection with the murder of Brigitta the harpy. The information you have provided is extremely useful, and we shall, of course, let you know when we apprehend the murderer.'

The harpy leaned forward making Ned nervous.

'You will tell me who your suspect is now, little

human.'

The door banged open, and Jenni returned, the fold-out table bobbing along behind her. Agatha turned to see who it was and immediately leapt to attention.

'Mistress Jenni! How may we serve?'

'You done 'ere, Boss?' asked Jenni.

Ned nodded.

'Get out of 'ere and don't eat nobody on your way 'ome!' Jenni dismissed the harpy who leapt out of the office.

'What was all that about?' asked Ned.

Jenni shrugged and set down the table. 'We had fing, they did stuff, I sorted it and now there ain't no fing.' She looked out the window at the disappearing harpy. 'She were quick.'

'Hmm, I think Sparks must have gone there first. Which means...' Ned was interrupted by a heavy footfall coming towards them down the corridor.

'Golem.' Ned and Jenni said to each other. She scooted over to the far side of the office, joining Willow whose trembling was creating a nervous rustling sound. Golems cared little for nature. Ned was still deciding whether to stand up or not when the door crashed open and the clay man entered.

I AM HERE TO ANSWER FOR THE CRIME OF MURDERING 27.

'Ah, hello. Thank you for responding so quickly. Won't you sit down?'

NO

'Probably for the best,' muttered Ned, eyeing the golem and the chair. 'Can you confirm your numb... er... name please?'

I AM 42.

'And can you confirm the name of the golem that

was destroyed?'

GOLEM 16 WAS RECENTLY DESTROYED IN THE MINES OF MR. SKIFFLE. GOLEM 36 WAS RECENTLY DESTROYED IN THE WORKSHOP OF THE ALCHEMIST PETRI. GOLEM 4 WAS RECENTLY DESTROYED BY CARELESS MACHINERY OPERATION AT THE DOCKYARD. GOLEM 27 WAS RECENTLY DECONSTRUCTED TO RUBBLE. ALL DESTRUCTIONS HAVE BEEN REPORTED TO MOMMA K IN ACCORDANCE WITH FAE REGULATIONS.

Jenni whistled. 'That's a lot of destruction.'

WE ARE EASILY REPLACEABLE THEREFORE CARE IS NOT TAKEN.

'We would like to know more about the golem that was recently deconstructed to rubble. Number 27,' prompted Ned.

YES. I AM HERE TO PLEAD NOT GUILTY FOR THAT DESTRUCTION.

'Plea accepted 42. We never thought you murdered one of your own, however, we would like to know any details surrounding that destruction.' Ned waited. 'If it's not too much trouble.' He waited some more. 'Any tiny detail could help our investigation.'

Everyone was watching to see whether the golem would speak. It was hard to tell if it was thinking or not. Ned tapped his pen on his paper and began humming as he waited for a response. He was trying to figure out how to move the golem from their office when it shifted slightly.

WE WERE RECENTLY VISITED BY A GOLEM FROM ANOTHER TOWN. THIS IS NOT UNUSUAL. WORK OPPORTUNITIES ARE MANY AND VARIED IN ROSHAVEN. IT IS GOOD TO BE A

GOLEM HERE.

'Okay, and did this visiting golem have any distinguishing marks?'

ITS CREATOR HAD CARVED A NEAT MOUSTACHE UPON THE FACE. SUCH ATTEMPTS TO HUMANISE GOLEMS ARE USUALLY NOT MADE.

'Is this golem still with you?'

NO. HE MUST HAVE RETURNED TO HIS PREVIOUS TOWN OF OWNERSHIP. WE DO NOT KNOW WHERE.

'Thank you very much for your time, 42.'

I HAVE MORE INFORMATION.

'Oh? Right. Carry on then.' Ned poised his pen above the pad and waited.

The golem's head slowly turned to fully face Ned, the unnatural eyes shining, lit from its crimson life fire within.

SILVERY DISCHARGE WAS FOUND AT THE SCENE OF THE RUBBLE. THIS IS NOT SOMETHING GOLEMS HAVE WITHIN THEM.

Ned coughed nervously. 'Right. Good to know. Thank you very much. Is there, er, anything else?'

NO

'Excellent. You are free to go.'

YOU WILL INFORM US OF THE OUTCOME OF YOUR INVESTIGATION.

'Yes, yes, we will. Most definitely.'

The golem turned and pounded its way back along the corridor, downstairs, and presumably out of The Noose. As they didn't eat or drink, unless ordered to do so for the amusement of their foreman, there was no reason why the golem would hang around.

Ned sighed in relief. 'Well, that was intense, eh?'

'Do you still need to speak to the uvvers, Boss?'
asked Jenni.

'I would like to corroborate all the facts. We do after
all have our moustache theme.'

'Yeah, 'spose.'

Sparks flew in the open window, buzzing and
flashing like a disco ball on high speed.

'What is it? What's happened? Jenni?' Ned gestured
for her to translate as the firefly alighted on her hand.

'Pixies ain't coming. They frettened to pull off 'is
wings. Cheeky little blinders! 'ere, s'awright Sparko,
they ain't gonna get you.'

Ned sighed. He would've liked to hear from the
pixies direct but the paperwork Momma K had supplied
did mention a sly pixie called Arnie who had a
moustache, so the *modus operandi* was still the same.

'Just the gingerbread people then, I guess.'

'They might take a while,' piped up Willow, pointing
out of the window. It had started to rain.

'Perhaps we should go see them. You coming,
Jenni?' Ned asked as he threw on his coat.

'Nah. I always wanna eat 'em. I'll stay 'ere, keep
fings ticking.'

'Willow?'

The wood nymph flowered at being asked and
sprang up from her chair then pouted. 'Will we be back
before four? Only I have my appointment...' She trailed
off as Ned nodded. Clapping her hands in happiness,
clouds of blossom erupted in various places.

'Okay, good. We'll be back soon. Joe?'

The lad looked up nervously.

'Do some filing. Jenni's in charge.' Joe nodded
vigorously as Ned held the door open for Willow. He
tried to ignore the sway of her hips on the stairs and the

smell of her perfume as she passed. Ned fingered his protective amulet and muttered a plea to any gods that were listening.

'Sorry, Boss.' Willow glanced back and saw Ned's rising blush. 'I'll try and prune it in.'

'Very good. Thank you, Willow. Right, come on. Let's go speak to the gingerbread people.' Ned turned the collar of his jacket up, ignoring the catcalls from the patrons that followed Willow out of the inn. They headed into the rain.

It wasn't far to the home of the gingerbread people. They lived in a quiet cul-de-sac on the north edge of the city. There were three cottages, but sadly only one of those had any occupants. Willow surveyed the gardens.

'I'm impressed. They keep their shrubbery well.'

'It's the flowerpot men,' replied Ned. 'They look after the fairy tale gardens. This is the only one left within the city limits now. Sad.'

They walked up to the door and Ned knocked three times.

'Just a minute!' came a crumbly voice. They waited on the damp porch, listening to shuffling and dragging noises coming from within. Finally, the door opened to reveal a gingerbread person.

'You're wet!' it shrieked. 'You can't bring that kind of moisture in. Please dry off in the vent.' It pointed to a plastic tube located on the inside of the cottage.

Ned and Willow dutifully stepped inside the tube and withstood a few seconds of hot air blasting at them from above and below. Willow's leaves all turned brown and she left a woodland trail as they walked through the hall to the kitchen.

'Are you alright?' whispered Ned.

Willow nodded and shook herself slightly, the rest of

the dead leaves falling off whilst new buds were already appearing.

In the kitchen, two gingerbread people were joined by the one who had opened the door. They sat on large chairs and smiled at their visitors. To be fair, they couldn't do anything else. They were iced that way. The delicious smell of gingerbread filled the room hinting at overtones of golden syrup and cloves. Ned told his stomach to do its best to ignore it.

'I'm very sorry for your loss,' he began but before he could continue, the largest of the gingerbread people, Man, spoke.

'We didn't kill Old Man Ginger. Just to be clear. And for you to accuse us with no evidence is biscuitism. We've already reported the crime to Momma K, she said she was dealing with it.'

The others nodded.

'I must apologise, I was trying to get several leading members of the fae community into the office to talk to me urgently and the quickest way to do that was to make them persons of interest wanted for questioning,' explained Ned.

'We have suffered a huge loss as well as trickery of the bake,' the gingerbread man crumbled on. 'An imposter had the nerve to pose as one of us, claiming he had the secret recipe to make more of our kind. But instead, he made these!'

Ned stared at the plate of biscuits on the table. They were indeed gingerbread men but the non-magical kind. 'Can you even eat them?' he murmured before raising his voice and asking the crucial question. 'Did he have a moustache? This imposter?'

All three gingerbread people nodded. 'How did you know? Have you caught him?' asked Man.

'Not yet, unfortunately, but we are working some important leads. Tell me, was there anything unusual at the scene of the murder?'

The baked goods crumbled ever so slightly.

'Any little detail could help us catch him,' Ned said encouragingly.

'Well... he didn't leave anything behind, if that's what you mean. But he... he... he'd dunked him and... and... eaten some!' wailed the smallest of the gingerbread people.

Ned was stunned. This was the furthest the murderer had gone, actually eating part of his victim. Yes, it was a gingerbread person, but Old Man Ginger had been alive for decades. That biscuit must have been fusty and musty and not very tasty at all.

'Can you give me any more information? A name? Details of where they went?' asked Ned.

'Called himself Arnouldi, which we thought then was a ridiculously overblown name, and he had that moustache what you mentioned. Very sure of himself, always watching, watching, watching and the lies he told. Shocking it was. Tried to tell Ginger here that cronuts were a thing. Have you ever heard of anything so ridiculous?' said Man.

Ned stayed quiet. He had tried one of Aggie's cronuts dipped in sugar. It wasn't as good as her cinnamon twists but it had definitely hit the spot.

'You don't seem overly upset, if you don't mind my saying,' said Willow softly. 'Were you expecting Grandfather to pass over soon?'

'It's hard to get attached to things when you're all biscuit, my dear. And yes, Grandfather was very stale, he'd lost one leg already and his buttons. It's a sad thing when a gingerbread person has lost their buttons.' It stared wistfully at Willow. 'You haven't seen the magical recipe, have you?'

'No, I'm sorry, I haven't.'

'Well if there's nothing else...' Man heaved himself to standing.

'Could we take those?' Ned pointed to the biscuits on the table. 'For evidence.'

Ginger scooted the plate over to Ned and he patted his pockets for a bag. There was a rustle behind him, and Willow gave him a fresh green one.

'What's that made of?' he asked.

'It's hemp. Long lasting, natural fibres,' she beamed. Ned decided not to question further and instead dropped the biscuits into the bag.

'Thank you for your time. Again, we are very sorry for your loss,' he said and bowed his head at the three gingerbread people and then headed for the door, Willow in his wake.

As they walked back to HQ, he opened the bag and drew out a biscuit.

'You're not actually going to eat those, are you, Boss?' asked Willow.

Ned replied by chomping down noisily and then spluttering as the dry biscuit crumbs made him cough. Not so nice after all.

# Chapter 6

'What is dis?' Momma K demanded as the leaders of the fae council approached her toadstool.  'Me did no call ya here?' A light breeze wafted across the smell of burnt caramel.

'Er... no. We're um... here because - well, you see - the thing is,' stammered Sylvan, the elf representative. He was nudged encouragingly by Fjorn the dwarf, while Egger the goblin and Penni the sprite kept a safe distance from Momma K, half-hidden behind the larger fae.

'They're 'ere cos they fink you is weak,' announced Jenni, who had popped into the fae glen unnoticed. She stomped over to stand with Momma K.

'Yes, that's it,' said Sylvan, feeling relief and then terror as he realised what he'd agreed to. 'N... n-no, that's n... n-not what I m... m-meant...'

Momma K cut him off with a wave of her hand. Her eyes flashed. The sky turned deep purple. 'Me no weak,' she hissed.

The council members inched closer together. Each of them represented a group of smaller fae creatures. Sylvan looked after the interests of the elves, pixies, nixies and various nymphs because there were too many iterations for them to each have a chair on the council. The pixies and nixies had set up camp in the enchanted wood, interrupting the elven peaceful existence, until the elves had finally agreed to speak to Momma K. Now that he had her attention, Sylvan was regretting that decision.

'It were the harpies that sent us,' squeaked Egger. He

hadn't meant to squeak; nerves were getting the better of him. Usually, the council met twice monthly for a catch-up and an occasional bake-off. They weren't accustomed to actually having to deal with a problem in the wider community.

Penni fidgeted and glanced nervously at Jenni. Officially, Penni was the sprite representative on the fae council but Jenni was Momma K's daughter, and she had more power at her fingertips than any other sprite. It all became too much for Penni and she discreetly popped away. Only Jenni noticed at first. It took a few moments for the rest of the council to catch on. Once they'd realised they were one member short, they huddled together even closer.

'Well? Tell me me weakness?' demanded Momma K.

'It's the murders, innit?' Jenni asked them.

They all nodded back vehemently.

Jenni turned to Momma K. 'It ain't their fault. They've bin asked to come.'

The sky lightened a shade, but the council seemed very unsure as to what was going to happen next.

Jenni took pity on them. 'Awright guys, you can go. I got this.'

'Er...' Fjorn cleared his throat excessively. 'We've been asked to remind Momma K that everything can be replaced.' He ducked but when no answering fireball hit him, he risked a glance. 'We're just the messengers.'

'Yeah, we know,' replied Jenni.

With relief, the representatives swiftly left.

Jenni flicked her fingers at the sky, and it returned to its more normal azure blue with a few lazy clouds drifting on by. 'Is this what you meant 'bout the reckoning?'

Momma K nodded. 'Me understand why dey came. Murders can no be left unpunished. It been too long already but me no bein' replaced. No yet.'

'Awright, wot plan you got then?'

Momma K inspected her fingernails for some time.

'I fink we need to trap 'im. Shapeshifters are greedy, right? So, let's lure 'im in wiv summik.'

Momma K wrinkled her delicate brow, tapping one finger on her lips. 'Chil', ya may be onta ting. But it needs to be public spectacle. Him will want to get away wid it.'

'Wot you finking then, some kinda tournament or race? Mebbe a game?'

'A game,' mused Momma K. 'A game could work. What games do dey play for money?'

Jenni laughed. 'You can play anyfink for money. We need to do summik wiv stakes. Summik you can bet on.'

'Snail racing? Parcheesi?'

'No one plays Parcheesi. It's gotta be summik that'll appeal to uvvers s'well.' Jenni paced up and down before spinning triumphantly to face Momma K. 'I got it! Poker!'

'A competition in poking? Dis what ya tink we should do?'

'Not poking, poker. It's a card game. Wot it is, right, is you bet on the cards wot you can't see and try and psyche out the uvver players into betting all their stuffs against you cos they fink they're gonna win, right?'

'Ya will play and ya will beat him.'

'Nah, wot we should do is put me in as the muscle. I can stop 'im if he tries anyfink. And if we make it a non-magical building then it's no funny business.'

'But ya will be wi'out ya magic. How doh dat make it fair game?' asked Momma K.

Jenni cracked her knuckles. 'I got ways.'

'Me will have to ask permission from dere emperor if we want to play de game out dere.' She waggled her fingers in the direction of the non-fae world.

'Really?' Jenni was surprised. 'Why?'

'We can do it anyway. But, for de look of tings, asking is best. Only... me need ya help, chil'.'

'Wiv wot?'

'Me need ya to get me audience wid de emperor. Me been... forbidden from visitin'.'

'K, well I can do that, 'spose. I'll 'ave to ask Ned to do it, they won't speak to me on me own.'

Momma K sniffed but said nothing.

'E knows you bin spying on 'im an'all.'

'Me jus' keeping eye on tings.'

'Yeah, well, we don't need no more of 'em. I got enough eyes for everyone.'

There was a brief pause as mother and daughter stared fiercely at each other, neither one blinking. Finally, Momma K inclined her head minutely. There would be no more fae spies.

'So, we make a non-magic place for the game, get some players in there and then trap 'im. Should be easy enuff. We gonna let Ned catch 'im? On account of the no magic fing?' asked Jenni.

'Me t'ought ya could handle it?'

'I can, I fink. But you know, for the look of fings.'

Momma K scowled. 'If him puts in de entry fee, him can apprehend de killa.'

'Wot's the entry fee?'

'Ten t'ousand gold bits,' replied Momma K calmly.

'Ten fousand! That's mental!'

'Me want to entice de shapeshifta. Greed will motivate him. Me met dere kind befoh,' remarked

Momma K darkly.

Jenni decided to save that conversation for later. She needed to think of a way to help Ned get ten thousand gold bits.

'Ya will no help de catcha,' said Momma K.

'Wot? I didn't say nuffink.'

'Ya doh' have to. Me warning ya, chil'. Doh help him in dis.'

Jenni huffed while scuffing the ground with her foot. 'I dunno why you is so off 'im.'

'Me want fae justice!' hissed Momma K. 'Go, get me audience wid de emperor. It past time we catch de murdera.'

'Yes, Momma K.' Jenni popped out.

# Chapter 7

Ned arrived back at the same time as Jenni and they entered The Noose together. Willow had flowered on to her important fertilisation appointment.

'The gingerbread people confirmed the specific crime details. A new person turned up with an iced moustache and disappeared after the murder.' Ned glanced at Jenni. 'Where've you been?'

'Momma wants a favour.'

'Oh, does she now? Are you going to tell me who the murderer is?'

Jenni pursed her lips and shook her head mutely.

'Then I don't think there is anything I can do.' Ned pushed past her and headed upstairs to HQ. Jenni hurried after him.

'Please, Boss!'

'Don't you *please, Boss* me. We are standing on the brink of losing an entire species of very important biscuitry thanks to some mental moustached murderer who you know the identity of but will not tell me about!' Ned was breathing hard, partly because he was angry and partly because he'd taken the stairs too fast.

'We've gotta way of catching 'im. Only Momma K needs to speak wiv the emperor.'

'So? Go speak to him then.' Ned threw his jacket at his chair, missed and toppled a pile of paperwork.

'We ain't allowed in no more.' Jenni shoved her hands into the pockets of her dirty red coat. 'You gotta ask for us.'

'I gotta ask for you?' Ned paced up and down his

office, various retorts swirling around his head. 'You know what? You know what?' He wagged a finger at her and then seemed to lose all his puff. 'Alright, fine. I'll ask for an audience. But I want in on the meeting. No more cutting me out.'

Jenni nodded enthusiastically. 'Yes, Boss. Of course, Boss. Anyfing you say, Boss.'

'They probably won't see us today anyway, it's coming up on tea-time,' said Ned as he double checked the empty pizza boxes one more time, just in case.

Ned tapped his foot in irritation. He'd done what they'd asked and come cap in hand to the palace requesting an audience with the Emperor. As Chief Thief-Catcher, he had the right. But, as a commoner with holes in his boots, he shouldn't have the audacity. He'd stuck his neck out and grovelled before the High Right Inquisitor and the High Left Lord Chamberlain, who'd passed his request on to the Upper Circle, and now he sat outside a meeting room. Not the second best or his usual haunt, the third best, but the actual, proper, formal room they used for dignitaries and other important people. The palace guards outside the closed doors ignored him. Ned fumed to himself and surreptitiously cast a simple eavesdrop spell, pulling on the reserves in his power well. The magic wobbled towards the doors, unnoticed by the guards, but dissolved as soon as it touched them. Obviously an anti-eavesdrop spell was in place. Ned fumed some more. What did he have to show for sticking his neck out? A seat outside the meeting room while her nibs spoke to her other nibs. What he wouldn't give to be a fly on that wall.

'Your Eminence.' Momma K formally inclined her

head in greeting.

'Your Majesty.' The emperor did the same. Robed in purple and wearing a golden mask that hid their face entirely, they were sitting on a gilded throne atop a raised dais. All around the room were displays of paintings, artefacts, sculpture and weaponry. Some had historic value to Roshaven, others were gifts from neighbouring kingdoms.

There was something in their response to her that made Momma K pause, frown and then smile to herself. She laughed softly and nodded as she glided closer.

'How may we help you?' asked the emperor.

'Me want to catch a murdera,' replied Momma K.

'An honourable pursuit. I have excellent thief-catchers.'

'Me doh' wantcha thief-catchas. Me want permission to hold tournament. A poker tournament.'

It was hard to tell behind the emperor's expressionless mask, but there was potential frowning.

'How will this help matters?'

'Me know who de murdera is. Me have a plan to catch him. But me need to hold de game in dis world. On dis plane. Specific, on de Dead Pier. It a powaful nexus.'

'Your fae murderer is killing my citizens. Can you not restrain your people?'

'Ya rules and regulations make it hard for us to operate in de city.'

'And having this tournament will guarantee catching the killer?'

'Me believe so.'

'On the Dead Pier. In what? A hut?'

Momma K nodded, and the emperor snorted.

'I have heard a lot of... discussion recently about fae leadership and whether a change might be brewing. My first duty is to the protection of *my* citizens.'

Momma K put her hands on her hips in indignation. 'Dere is no change comin' in ya lifetime. Believe on dat!' she said, shaking her head slightly. She held her hands out, palm up and entreated. 'Help me catch dis killa and de city will be safe. A new fae ruler might have... designs.'

The emperor inclined their head benevolently. 'I'll agree to the tournament on one condition.'

'Yes?' Momma asked warily.

'You set the buy-in price too high for the majority of my citizens to enter, and I get fifty percent of the profits. For the good of the empire.'

'Ten percent.'

'Fifty.'

'Fifteen.'

The emperor shifted slightly on their throne. 'Fifty-five.'

Momma K smiled again. 'Aite. Have ya fifty percent. And de buy-in will be high. Ten t'ousand gold bits high.'

'That should be deterrent enough. I don't want any more citizens hurt in the apprehension of this vile person.'

'Dat is somet'ing we can boat agree on.'

There was a pause in negotiations. Both leaders waited for the other to speak first.

'Will you be dealing out justice?'

Momma K smiled slowly. 'Believe.'

'No assistance needed?' asked the emperor. 'We have very deep dungeons.'

'Dat will no be needed. Fae justice will suffice.'

'Very well. I shall inform my thief-catchers they are not to take part in this game. Unless of course, a law is broken. One must uphold the law.'

Momma K flexed her wings slightly. 'Of course.'

'Your Majesty.'

'Your Eminence.'

The two figures bowed respectfully before Momma K gracefully left the room. Ned leapt to his feet on her reappearance.

'Everything alright?' he asked.

Momma K sniffed at him in disapproval then glided out of sight. Ned turned back to the meeting room doors, but they were firmly closed. He dithered, not knowing whether he was free to go. In the end, it was the smirk from the palace guard on the left-hand side of the doors that decided him. He stomped off out of the palace and met Jenni outside.

'I don't appreciate being used like this,' Ned said. 'They wouldn't even let me into the meeting and Momma K disappeared without telling me what happened.

'Sorry, Boss. You just missed 'er.' Jenni pointed helpfully in the direction Momma K had flown.

'That doesn't help me now. I suppose you know what was said?'

'Yeah, basically. Momma K told me on 'er way past. The emperor said it were awright so we're going for it.'

'Going for what, exactly?' asked Ned, feeling grumpy.

'A poker tournament.'

'A what?'

'You know, it's a game wiv cards wot you play for money.'

'Yes, thank you, Jenni. I know what a poker game is. Where will the game be held – not in the palace?'

'Nah, on the Dead Pier. Inna hut.'

'A hut?'

'Yep.'

They walked up the cobbled street in silence for a while before Ned asked more questions.

'When exactly is this poker game meant to be happening? And who is meant to be playing in it? Do you really think a game will catch your murderer?'

'Tomorrow, those wot buy-in and yeah, fink so. He's a greedy sod so 'e won't be able to stay away.'

'Who is he, Jenni?'

'Dunno 'zactly, Boss. Honest I don't.'

'Hmm. Don't you think tomorrow is a bit quick? How will anyone know about it?'

'I'm gonna go see Neeps. Get 'er to put it in the rag and then thems wot wanna play can come straight over on the day.'

'What if you don't get any players?'

'We will.'

'Jenni? What's the buy-in?' Ned had a bad feeling.

'Ten fousand gold bits.'

Ned whistled softly. He couldn't think of many Roshaven residents who would have enough coin to play, but there were a couple that sprang to mind: the dwarves obviously, and possibly the gnomes as well. The trolls didn't go in for gold, and he doubted the druids would have that much lying around. He couldn't think of any human players except for maybe Lady Shillot, but she didn't seem like a betting person.

'You'd better get over to *The Daily Blag*. Neeps will be finishing off the late edition soon. And if you actually want people to hear about this game, you need to get the ad in the paper.'

'You gonna play, Boss?' asked Jenni.

'Are you joking? I haven't got money like that. Besides, thief-catchers are meant to uphold the law, not gamble for gold.'

'But if you did. 'ave the gold I mean.'

'No, Jenni. Our job would be to arrest him, not play cards with him. So if he does turn up, we'll be ready.'

'Momma K wants fae justice.'

'And I want to catch a murderer.'

'But it ain't your fing. That's why she's left you out o' stuff.'

Ned stopped walking. 'As thief-catchers, we have a duty to our emperor and our city to apprehend and detain those breaking the law. You are a thief-catcher, Jenni, and I expect you to do your duty tomorrow and wait with me to catch this murderer.' He peered at the sprite. 'You don't have ten thousand gold bits, do you?'

'Nah. Well, mebbe, I dunno, but I ain't no good at card games so I ain't entering. The game that is.' She tried once more. 'Boss, can't you just let this one go? He ain't gonna get away wiv it.'

'No, he is not.' Ned's stomach grumbled. 'I'd hurry if I were you, Neeps will be printing the paper soon. It's almost tea-time.'

'Yeah, awright. See you tomorrow, Boss.' And Jenni popped over to *The Daily Blag* office leaving Ned to walk home, alone.

# Chapter 8


'Awright Neeps?' asked Jenni as she walked into the brightly lit office of *The Daily Blag*. Inside there were a couple of tables with scattered sheets of paper on them and a few unmatched chairs. The newspaper didn't have a huge staff and Neeps usually managed on her own.

'What can I do for you?' The reporter was surprised to see the fae catcher. Usually, Jenni avoided the press like the plague.

'I need you to do an advert. For a fing.'

'What thing?' Neeps was wary. 'Who's paying for the advert?'

Jenni clicked her fingers and a bag of gold coins appeared on the desk.

'They'd better not be made of chocolate.' Neeps poked them with the end of her pen. They chinked delightfully.

Jenni snort-laughed which made Neeps smile.

'Okay, what do you want to advertise?'

'It's a poker tournament. 'appening on the Dead Pier this Friday, at midday. Buy-in is ten fousand gold coins.'

'Tomorrow! You've left it a bit late.' Then she did a double take. 'Ten thousand gold coins! No one will be able to pay that.' Neeps narrowed her eyes at Jenni. 'What's this really about? Is this a trap for the murderer?'

'I ain't saying nuffink,' replied Jenni but she touched her nose with her index finger and gave Neeps a wink.

'You won't get many players with a buy-in like that. Especially leaving it 'til the last minute to tell everyone about it.'

'We'll get enuff. Are you gonna run it or wot?'

Neeps nodded. 'I can make space on the front page. Besides the murders, it's been a slow news week. Who's the contact? You?'

'Nah. Just say bring the gold to the hut on the Dead Pier tomorra if you want in and we'll sort it.'

Neeps nodded as she made notes. 'One last question, is this Emperor-approved? I'm not going to get in trouble for printing this, am I?'

Jenni shook her head. 'It's all bin sorted, no problem. Fanks, Neeps.' And she popped out leaving Mariah Neeps staring at the bag of gold coins, waiting for them to disappear too. After five minutes she poked them again and they still chinked. Feeling a good deal happier, Neeps whistled cheerily as she put together the advertising copy.

INTERSPECIES POKER TOURNAMENT
TOMORROW ~ 12 O'CLOCK
AT THE DEAD PIER

BUY-IN 10,000 GOLD COINS

*Bring your gold to the Dead Pier to enter – good luck!*

Neeps looked over the copy. It didn't look very exciting, but it had all the information Jenni had given her. She decided to replace the entire front page with the advert, that way no one would miss it and hopefully, enough players would turn up to the event. *I'll definitely be in the audience* thought Neeps, *a high stakes poker game and a plan to catch a murderer should make a great news story.* She hummed happily as she set the printing plates. The printing press that produced *The Daily Blag* was enchanted thanks to a dodgy deal Neeps' father had managed to wangle with Momma K. Something to do with a lifetime subscription and jam. The printing press could produce the new edition in next to no time. While the press swung into clanging, banging action, amidst the smell of paper and ink and the heavy clunk of completed sheets being ejected, Neeps went to tell the paper sellers to specifically shout about the tournament. It wouldn't be long before Roshaven knew all about it.

# **Chapter 9**

'Wot would you do wiv the moolah, then?' asked Jenni.

The Interspecies Poker Tournament was the hot topic of conversation as Jenni, Willow, Joe and Sparks patrolled their usual morning beat around Roshaven - past their favourite eateries, with a turn around the minuscule green, and an extremely wide berth for the Black Narrows. A pickpockets' dream, they were exactly as described, narrow alleys in black stone. No one went into the Black Narrows voluntarily, unless they were naive tourists or had the misfortune to live there. And if you did live there, you didn't go out in the narrows at night unless you absolutely had to and even then, you'd try to get out of it.

Of course, for some, it was part of their professional workload to be in the narrows, especially at night. It was one of *those* places, a tourist honey trap for people seeking danger, and suitable living conditions for those wishing to cause the danger. The thief-catchers were only being sensible in their patrol, there was asking for trouble and then there was begging for it.

'I'd buy my own orchard,' said Willow wistfully. As a tree nymph it was the obvious choice. 'And build a water park.' That, on the other hand, was not.

'Wot about you, Sparks?' asked Jenni.

The firefly went on a highly convoluted display of flashes, pulses and zips, finally coming to an exhausted stop in a handy piece of foliage Willow was currently experimenting with as her hair.

All eyes turned to Jenni.

'Wot? Oh, right. 'e says a new place for 'is family.'

'Was that all? He seemed to go on a bit for just that.' Joe scratched his ear.

'Yeah, well, obvs 'e talked about the towers and the moat and that, you know, all the extra fings, but I boiled it down. Translator's discretion.'

The others nodded. Firefly language could be hard to interpret at times.

'I'd get my own place and maybe ask that waitress out.' There was no need to ask who Joe meant. He used to moon over a certain waitress all the time, but the restaurant she worked in was now off limits to all thief-catchers. There had been a disagreement about fees. And so, the catchers had released the restaurant thief together with all his takings and their very best wishes. It hadn't gone down well with the establishment owner. Joe was no longer welcome in the restaurant, and he hadn't even had the chance to ask her name before he'd been barred. She was just known as *the waitress*.

'All solid choices,' Jenni commented as they swung into Palace Lane, nearing the end of their morning beat.

'What would you do?' Willow was trailing tendrils and encouraging all the little weeds in-between the cobbles to flourish.

'It's a ten-fold plan, see. First...' But they never got to find out as Ned met them halfway down the lane.

'Good, I found you. Willow, Joe, Sparks, I need you to go see Mr. Miller. He claims his neighbour has been stealing apples from his tree, but I suspect it may be tricks from one of your mates.' He looked at Willow and she flushed greenly before ushering the others off to deal with the situation.

'All quiet, Jenni?'

'Yes, Boss. We was talking about wot we'd do if we

won.'

'Won what?'

'The interspecies poker tournament.'

'Well, you don't need to worry about that, Jenni. It's not for the likes of us. Only those who pay that extortionate buy-in fee are granted access to the table. Besides, the Emperor doesn't want anyone in law enforcement involved in the game.'

'Why not?' Jenni kicked a stone a little too vigorously. It ricocheted off a lamp post and flew back at them, whizzing past Ned's ear.

'Something to do with conflict of interest. There was a note on the door of HQ – didn't you see it?'

There was no reply.

'Everything alright?' Ned asked as they arrived at The Noose. Jenni was uncharacteristically on time this morning and had volunteered to do the morning beat, she never volunteered. For anything. Except if it was food related.

She didn't answer him and instead peeled off towards the bar muttering, 'I'm gonna get summik to drink.'

Ned frowned. Jenni didn't drink alcohol. He convinced himself that she was probably getting one of those sugar-laden coffees she enjoyed so much. It was on her insistence that Reg started serving coffee in The Noose. The barman had been resistant to the idea until, suddenly, he wasn't; Ned hadn't investigated. He went up the rickety stairs to their office. She'd tell him when she was good and ready.

He opened the door. The office was full of water. He shut the door quickly in case he triggered a flood. When he realised there was no water on the floor, he opened it again and considered the possibilities. A small shoal of fish glinted past the doorway. The water was definitely in the office and yet it was not spilling out. He cautiously poked a finger into the suspended liquid. Yep, definitely water. He licked his finger. *Huh, briny.* Either he was hallucinating, or the sea had drowned his office.

'Jenni!'

With a greasy pop, she appeared beside him, sans coffee.

'Yes, Boss?'

'Why is my office full of seawater?' asked Ned.

'Is it?' Jenni took a look. An octopus, who looked very familiar, was idly filing Ned's paperwork which had previously covered the entire top of his desk, several chairs and parts of the floor. Realising he was being watched, the cephalopod gave a sort of undulating shrug somehow indicating through tentacle mime that it wanted to be useful. Six of its limbs continued opening and closing drawers. It was clearly a magical flood as the paperwork seemed unaffected by the presence of water, yet the octopus was very much in his element.

'Er, I dunno, Boss,' said Jenni. 'Could be fing.'

'Fing?'

'Yeah, you know. One of 'em wotsits.' Jenni wiggled a finger in her ear waxily as she perused the oceanic scene. 'A sign of impending doom or summik.'

Ned grunted. 'I hardly think my office being full of water is a sign of impending doom.'

'S'pose it depends if you can swim, Boss.'

There was a clanging noise behind them. The two thief-catchers turned to see Fred, an earnest young palace guard, making his way up the staircase. Unaware he was being watched, he paused at the top to catch his breath, after having run all the way from the Emperor's Palace. His official plume dangled in front of his face, point blank refusing to sit upon his helmet erectly. After pushing it out of his eyes three times by puffing what little breath he had left at it, Fred gave up.

Jenni hawked a spitball, making Fred jump and his helmet wobble precariously on top of his head, sending the plume dancing.

'Oh! You gave me a fright, Miss Jenni. Mr. Spinks, Sir. Only I ran all the way and... bit puffed out... cos you know... they're doing the works... over on Didcot and you can't get through... unless you've got a pass but... I don't have one... on account of our Brian.' Fred beamed then looked behind them at the open door. Having caught his breath, he ventured a question. 'Er, why is your office full of water? It hasn't rained since last Thursday. Are you under a geas? Me mam says you have to be terrible careful of them. Cause all sorts of trouble they do.' He waved at the octopus who tentacled back. 'What you been up to then? Anything good?' He looked at them expectantly.

Jenni turned to Ned. The octopus also seemed riveted, waiting for an explanation. It was his day off from Sea Precinct and he had been expecting to spend his morning crawling through impossibly small spaces in the underwater rock formation he lived in, but he wasn't complaining. A change was as good as a rest. He'd never worked in a land office before and was enjoying himself so much that he was thinking of requesting a work release.

'We haven't been up to anything, Fred. No geas's here.' Ned made a mental note to check exactly what a geas was. Just in case. 'Did you have a message for us? From the Emperor?'

Fred was too fascinated by the office aquarium to reply. It was the closest he'd ever been to real, live fish besides the battered kind down on Carnaby Row and he was fairly sure those had never seen the ocean.

'Fred!' shouted Ned making the poor lad yelp and jump.

Casting a wounded look at him, Fred took out a small scroll from his messenger pouch and began to read. 'The Emperor - *may he live for ever and ever* - reminds the Thief-Catchers that gambling is most definitely frowned upon. And if anyone in law enforcement is found entering the Interspecies Poker Tournament, any winnings will be confiscated for the good of the empire.' Fred looked thoughtful for a moment. 'That's a bit rum, ain't it? No point in playing if you can't win.'

'And a good lesson to learn, Fred. Now, if that's all, we've got a lot of work to do,' said Ned, gently shushing the young guard down the stairs.

He went very obediently. Sheep-like qualities were highly sought after in his occupation.

'I wonder why the emperor don't want you to play, Boss?' asked Jenni. She had been hoping the emperor would tell Ned to take part, especially as she couldn't give him the buy-in without risking the wrath of Momma K.

'Never mind that, I've figured out why my office is full of water.' Ned took out his notepad, scribbled a brief message, and then looked around until he spied an empty beer bottle over by the stairwell. There were some advantages to having your office located above a pub. Sticking the note in the bottle, he lobbed it into his office where it floated about for a bit before gradually falling through the water. As it fell, the liquid level in the room went down until there was nothing left except a small puddle in the middle on the floor, a rather distraught octopus and the distinct smell of seaweed. There was no other evidence that the room had recently been flooded, not a single bead of water, and the bottle had vanished. 'Jenni, take him back to the ocean.' Ned pointed at the octopus. 'I'll meet you at the Dead Pier, at the Drop Off. I need to grab something first,' and he marched into the room.

'Rightchoya, Boss,' said Jenni. 'Er... why are you going to the drop off? I fink it's gonna be busy over there today, what wiv the game an' all.' Jenni was doing her best to sound casual and nonchalant. It wasn't working very well but Ned was too distracted to notice.

'This is mermaid magic,' he said, waving his arm around the room. 'Their way of saying *we need to talk.* I'll meet you there, okay?'

'Yeah, but I gotta do summik at midday.'

'Fine, fine.' Ned was checking the shelf where various odds and ends had been left and not really listening.

Jenni waited a moment, shrugged, and then popped herself and the bewildered octopus out of sight.

Now that the majority of his filing had been done, Ned could see the surface of his desk and there, poking out from under a stack of handbooks, was his anti-mermaid amulet. You could never be too careful when dealing with those vicious bloodsuckers. If you thought sharks were the most dangerous creature in the ocean, you'd obviously never met a hungry mermaid. He popped the amulet over his neck then had a second thought. Another bottle and scrap of parchment were swiftly found and used. Smiling, Ned hurried out of the office and down the stairs. A quick nod over to Reg let the barman know there was no one left upstairs. Usually, Reg did a good job of stopping unwanted visitors unless it was a slow night, then he invited any regulars upstairs for a general poke around. Ned was sure that was why they never had any pens.

# Chapter 10

It wasn't far to the Dead Pier. It was one of the more interesting tourist attractions Roshaven had to offer, on account of being constructed completely out of bones. Skulls hung at jaunty angles along railings made of femurs and tibias. Some of the skulls were painted blood red, others black but most had been bleached white and were highly polished. They all had deep, empty, eye sockets and grinning teeth.

The Dead Pier was a place to pay tribute to a loved one. Back in the day, it had been respectful to leave a bone behind. Indeed, the original wooden construction of the pier had been overlain with lashed together ribs, legs and arm bones so many times, it was hard to tell whether any wood remained. It was considered far too provincial these days to simply add to the pier with any old bone, instead, only skulls were left behind. At All Hallows, one lucky custodian had the honour of ensuring that all the skulls were strung across the width of the pier with candles flickering within them, creating a most atmospheric effect. The Emperor had allowed the pier to remain because it was a huge tourist attraction though health and safety turned up from time to time. These pencil pushers spent a great deal of time hemming and hawing before writing large reports recommending demolition of the pier. It was usually at this time that the local religious figureheads held meetings with the Emperor and things stayed just as they were. Having lots of bones in one spot created an excellent space for focused devotion, provided plenty of good juju, and demonstrated clearly the best way to honour your dead. Which included a large payment to your chosen place of worship.

The Drop Off, at the end of the pier, was the traditional spot to talk to the mermaids. That and the dangerous activity of taking your life into your own hands by leaping off the safety of hundreds of skeletal remains into the predator infested waters below. Particularly popular with the more daring Roshaven youth. Sea creatures lurked. Some lucky jumpers were fortunate to return with most of their limbs.

Jenni was already waiting for Ned when he arrived.

'All sorted?' asked Ned.

Not entirely sure what her boss was on about, Jenni squinted at him and scratched her nose.

'The octopus? Back in the water?'

'Oh yeah, 'e's all sorted.'

'Good. Right then, let's find out what's going on.' Ned sat down on the edge of the pier and took one of his trusty old boots off. Despite the rather large hole in his sock, Ned removed that as well. It was best to have full contact with the water when trying to get a mermaid's attention. He dipped his foot in cautiously and waggled his toes. He didn't have to wait long. A V-shape in the water accelerated towards him. He had barely lifted his foot out of the water before a large seal poked its head out of the waves.

'Er...' Ned was unsure of the correct etiquette in responding to a mermaid summons. 'We got your message. How can the Thief-Catchers help?'

The seal glared at him.

He thought frantically back to his academy days and the brief training he'd received on dealing with alternative species. Tread carefully had been the overall message, but Ned couldn't even do that on account of the whole water, land divide.

The seal tossed its head, breaking the animal glamour. A luscious mermaid revealed herself.

Ned felt the full force of her come hither attraction spell. The amulet he wore grew very hot, very fast, then burst into flames. Yelping in surprise, he scrabbled at the leather thong trying to rip it from his neck before the rest of him caught fire. Jenni conjured a bucket of water that she dumped over him, which was followed swiftly by the mermaid sweeping a huge wave of seawater at his face. Spluttering slightly, Ned coughed his thanks and gingerly patted his chest. The amulet briefly spat out some green sparks then let out a puff of steam, its destruction complete. Everything else on Ned's body seemed intact.

'Turn it down a bit, love. We're 'ere to 'elp, right? We ain't gonna eat you.' Jenni tried to placate the mermaid who looked a little startled by the amulet's pyrotechnics.

'Right, sorry. Habit. We don't get much interaction with non-mer these days. And after what happened...' She trailed off.

'Okay. Let's start again,' said Ned. 'I'm Ned Spinks, Chief Thief-Catcher. This is my second-in-command, Jenni. We got your message - thanks by the way - and we're here. So, why don't you tell us what happened.'

The mermaid waved her tail in the water as she considered how best to begin. 'We don't get many visitors. It's not that we're not friendly - we are! However, spending time underwater is difficult for most creatures without gills so hardly anyone makes the effort to get to know us. Then we had a shapeshifter visit.'

'A shifter? Wot, really?' Jenni interrupted. This could be the murderer. 'Ow do you know 'e was a shifter?'

The mermaid sniffed at being interrupted. 'Because he didn't come to us as a mermaid. He was something small, covered in cake crumbs. Anyway, this shapeshifter goes by the name of Armando, showed up wanting to get his mermaid likeness perfect.' The mermaid tossed her locks over one shoulder and fluttered her eyelashes at Ned. 'We're sirens of the sea you know, destined to lure men to their deaths with our haunting melodies. Naturally, we were flattered when someone wanted to take the time to understand us. Not many land people do.'

'Can't fink why,' Jenni muttered.

Ned shushed her.

'So, he came, and he spent some time with us and asked lots of questions. The next thing we knew, Clamella had been strangled and Armando was high-tailing it out of the water.' The mermaid shuddered at the memory.

'How do you know it was Armando who murdered Clamella - er, sorry, I didn't catch your name?' asked Ned.

'I'm Pearl,' she replied. 'And we knew because who else is going to strangle a mermaid?'

'A novver mermaid?' suggested Jenni.

Pearl glared at her.

'She does make a fair point, Pearl. It could've been another mermaid and not that *shapeshifter*. Do you have any evidence?' asked Ned.

'There was some kind of residue on the body, I can show you.'

Pearl dove beneath the waves. Ned and Jenni both peered cautiously over the side of the pier. A dead mermaid rose to the surface within a stasis bubble, protecting her from scavengers and decay. A trail of silvery fingerprints ran along the length of her faded red tail. Silver ooze crusted around the delicate mouth and nostrils of the extremely beautiful, very dead mermaid.

'Clamella, I presume?' asked Ned. 'A stasis bubble, is that normal mer-magic?'

Pearl nodded. 'It doesn't take long for the scavengers to gather.' She began keening softly, expressing her grief. Mermaids don't cry.

'Jenni, a word.' Ned cocked his head away from the body. He didn't know much about shapeshifters. He'd never come across one before, in training or in the field but everything was clicking into place. Of course his elusive murderer was a shapeshifter. 'Is this what Momma K didn't want me to know? That the murderer is a shapeshifter?'

'Yeah,' Jenni replied in a small voice.

Ned's voice dropped to an accusatory whisper. 'Why didn't you just tell me?'

'Momma K said it were too risky. She said if peoples knew what 'e was, they'd use 'im for stuffs and it'd be way worse.'

'Worse than a string of unsolved murders which, oh, let's double check – are all bloody related in that the same person murdered them!' He finally rose his voice.

Jenni flinched at being on the end of his wrath. Ned had never shouted at her like this.

'We will be discussing this further,' Ned said before he walked back to the side of the pier.

Jenni trailed morosely behind him.

'Sorry about that, Pearl. I needed to fact check with my colleague. Jenni, can you tell Pearl what you know about shapeshifters, please?'

'Well...' Jenni picked her nose thoughtfully, then rolled the findings and flicked them into the ocean, earning herself a look of disgust from Pearl. 'I ain't an expert and this is only wot Momma K told us when we was little, but as far as I can remember, that's classic shifter right there. They got silver in 'em - blood or mucus or substance or summik. And when they change, it gets all gunky and stuffs. They leaves bits. Surprised it ain't washed away though.'

'We put her in a stasis bubble as soon as we found her.' Pearl sniffed. 'If you don't mind, we'd like to commit her body to the ocean as soon as possible. I assume you've seen enough?'

'Not really, we need to see the crime scene. There might be some incriminating evidence. Is that still in stasis?' asked Ned.

Pearl nodded. 'I can't guarantee your safety; emotions are running cold. You might be the tail of dangerous pranks. Land authority doesn't have much sway.'

'Be that as it may, we only have your word for what happened. No offence.'

Pearl gazed at him fish-eyed.

'We need to see the scene, corroborate your allegations. Right, Jenni?'

'Er, yeah, 'spose.'

'Can you...' Ned wagged his fingers. 'Do the necessary, please?'

'Why ain't you doing it, Boss? You can spell this one, can't you?'

Ned scowled at her as he mentally reached deeply into his spell-casters belt. All he managed to pull out were a few gold sparks. As they fell from his fingers, they sputtered on the damp deck and disappeared.

'Yeah awright, I'll do it but I ain't going wiv though, Boss. I got that fing.'

Ned turned away from the mermaid and lowered his voice.

'We have a serious crime to investigate, Jenni. I need you to come down with me. The shapeshifter might still be swimming around. It'll take both of us to arrest him and besides, who else is going to do the time of murder spell?' He glared at her because she knew full well that he didn't have the spell-casting ability to do those.

'I can give you that, Boss. Just fling it when you get there but I ain't going.' Jenni shuffled her feet and picked wax out of her ear before continuing in a small voice. 'Momma K wants me to do summik else today.'

'What can possibly be so important that you can't come to a crime scene? Actually, you know what? I don't want to know. Sooner or later, Jenni, you are gonna have to decide whether you're catcher or fae. And you'd better seriously think about it. You're no good to me one leg in, one leg out.'

Jenni looked down at her legs and Ned breathed a sigh of exasperation.

'Not literally! Honestly, Jenni.' He shook his head. 'Can I have that spell, please?'

'Yeah. Sorry, Boss.' Jenni muttered something under her breath and created a blue glowing ball of energy. She then compressed it with her fingers until it resembled a shiny blue coin. 'Frow this at the scene and it'll do wot you want.' She handed it to him as she cast a dubious eye at Pearl, who was impatiently lashing her tail in the water. 'You gonna be alright down there, Boss? Can it not wait?'

'No, it cannot but I'll be fine. You go do whatever it is Momma K needs you for. I'll check in with you when I get back.'

'K.'

'Are you sure you're alright, Jenni?'

She nodded and leant over the side of the pier, glaring down at Pearl. 'Oi, fish breath. One 'air of 'is 'ead outta place and I'll 'ave you fried, wiv chips.'

'As long as he stays with me, nothing should happen to him,' retorted the mermaid. 'If he ever gets in the water, that is.'

'Right, yes. Er... Jenni? Before you go, could you gill me? Please?'

Jenni snapped her fingers.

Ned gasped for air. Clutching at his neck, he discovered that the gills were already in place. He gratefully fell inelegantly off the side of the pier and into the water. Glancing back at the decking he saw that Jenni had already disappeared.

'Are you ready?' asked Pearl. She had a secure hold on the deceased mermaid and the stasis bubble had clouded so it was difficult to see the body within.

Ned had to take a couple of deep breaths before he could respond. 'Lead the way.' He scrambled to follow the quickly disappearing tail. The fact that Pearl had Clamella with her made it slightly easier to keep pace with her. He could hear clicks and whistles from what he assumed was an assortment of marine life but he couldn't see any creatures nearby. The deeper they went the murkier the water became. It seemed to Ned that they were swimming into nothing. After what felt like the longest few minutes of his life, they reached a randomly placed set of rusty old gates.

'These are the gates to our town. If you stay with me, you should be fine. Make sure you keep away from the children. They're hungry.' Pearl swam through.

Ned gulped or at least tried to. When underwater, breathing liquid instead of air, the human body is mostly fighting the firm idea that it thinks it's drowning. He had heard rumours of the ferocity of merchildren and was in no rush to meet any.

There was an incredibly muscular merman on the other side of the gates who nodded to Pearl and flicked his tail gently so that it touched the cloudy bubble briefly. As Ned got closer to the entrance, the merman loomed, baring his way.

'He's with me, Derek. He's land authority.'

Derek grunted and drifted back. Ned had to swim past him, far closer than he wanted to. Passing through the gates, he entered into another world. A glamour was clearly in place. Before, Ned had seen nothing but gloom. Now, he saw neat rows of houses and a few merpeople here and there going about their business. He looked around nervously for any hungry children but couldn't see anything. With a start, he realised Pearl had swum away from him. He scrambled to catch up, creating a flurry of bubbles. When he pulled up next to them, his vigorous motion jostled the mermaid.

Pearl hissed at him.

Ned held his hands up in apology and tried to get his nerves under control.

She led him to one of the houses. It had a neat row of clam shells around the doorway.

'Clamella's place, I assume?'

'Yes.' Pearl went first into the house. The doorway opened immediately into a living space where the outline of a mermaid glowed in phosphorus. Pearl gently laid Clamella's stasis bubble within the outline and floated back so Ned could get on with his investigation.

He pulled the blue coin out of his pocket and threw it at the scene of the crime. At least he tried to. The coin, being small and light, took forever to float to the floor.

Ned couldn't think of a single thing to say to Pearl, so they waited in awkward silence. Finally, the coin landed, and the spell expanded. Blue power whooshed out and flooded the area, making it glow. A jumble of figures flew around as the time spell worked its magic.

'How is that supposed to help?' asked Pearl.

'The spell is going backwards until it finds the point of death. It will rewind the scenes prior and we should be able to see what happened.'

'I already told you what happened,' muttered Pearl. Ned chose to ignore her; the spell was slowing down.

# Chapter 11

Ned and Pearl watched in silence as Clamella floated around her house doing little bits of tidying and tending to her houseweed. She shooed out some crabs and was tackling a persistent starfish when she turned her head towards the door.

'That'll be the doorbell, then,' commented Ned. 'Do you have doorbells?'

'Doorshells.'

'Right.'

The front door in the vision opened. A middle-aged merman floated at the entrance. He had a white fishtail and a moustache which undulated gently in the current. Clamella smiled at her visitor and opened the door wider to allow him to swim in.

Nothing happened initially, they were just talking. Ned wished he could read lips. Jenni's spell came without sound. Pearl lashed her tail angrily. She could read lips.

'What? What happened?' asked Ned.

'That shifter, he asked Clamella how long her tail was. You never ask a merperson how long their tail is.'

Ned watched Clamella in the vision. 'She doesn't seem too bothered by it.'

'That's because she thought he was interested in her, scale and all. Such a jelly head.'

Clamella was definitely flirting, her tail flicked out to touch Armando's arm a couple of times and she played coyly with long locks of her hair. Finally, Armando leaned in for what looked like a kiss but turned out to be his kill.

Pearl gasped and turned away, but Ned kept watching. He couldn't understand why the shapeshifter had to kill his victims when he was already impersonating their shape. Once Armando had finished sucking the life out of Clamella, the silvery residue was immediately apparent around her mouth and Armando looked... more. It was as though he had become the embodiment of all things mer. He seemed more streamlined, more aquatic, like he'd spent all his life as a merman.

'Hmmm,' Ned said thoughtfully as the spell ended.

Pearl swam angrily through the dissipating blue energy. 'Do you believe me now?' she demanded of Ned.

'It was never about not believing you, Pearl. It was about trying to see the shapeshifter's process. He obviously gains something from killing his victim. It's not just a murder spree.' Realising that he was voicing his thoughts, Ned coughed to cover up his gaffe. At least he tried to cough but being underwater and not actually breathing air, all that he managed to do was create a large stream of bubbles.

'Are we done here?' asked Pearl.

Ned hesitated. 'Are you sure there has been no sign of him since you found Clamella's body?'

She shook her tail angrily and gestured for him to leave the house.

Ned swam out and followed her back to the gates. They passed through them and Pearl showed no sign of leaving Ned alone, so he had her company on the way back to the surface. He didn't mind. His body was beginning to rebel against Jenni's spell. His lungs were burning for air and the sides of his neck were prickling like mad. A quick feel with his fingers revealed the gills were closing, so he doubled his kicking effort and shot to the top of the water like a cork out of a bottle. He floundered about gasping as his body tried unsuccessfully to breathe air and water at the same time.

Through the waves and the splashing, he saw that Jenni was standing on the pier, but she had her back to him. It took Ned a couple of goes before he had enough puff to shout her name.

When she heard him, she spun around in surprise with a momentary guilty look on her face. 'Boss! Er... you awright?'

Ned tried to point to his neck, but moving his arms affected his limited buoyancy. He dipped under the water a couple of times before his body behaved itself and stopped trying to drown him. 'A little... help?' Ned managed to ask.

'Oh, yeah. Sorry, Boss.' Jenni snapped her fingers and Ned went from thrashing for air in the water to gasping for breath on the decking.

Pearl looked on in amusement.

'Wot 'appened to your gills?' asked Jenni.

Ned glared at her. 'They disappeared.'

'Did you not magically extend 'em?'

'I didn't know I had to.'

'Yeah. I musta forgot to tell you that bit, Boss.'

'Clearly.' Ned pushed himself up to sitting and thought about wringing his clothes out. Jenni had the same thought because the next minute he was feeling warm and tingly all over, thanks to her drying out spell. Ned leaned over to grab his boots and began putting his socks back on.

'So... was it then, Boss?' asked Jenni.

'Was it what?'

There was a loud splash. 'Look, I'm sorry to

interrupt, but when are you going to catch the murderer?' Pearl called from the water.

Ned opened his mouth to reply then closed it again. He wasn't exactly sure what to say as he didn't really know how they were going to catch the shapeshifter.

'Boss?'

'What, Jenni?'

'Was it?'

Ned glared at Jenni who innocently tipped her head sideways at him, waiting for him to answer.

'Yes, to all intents and purposes, it looks like a moustache wearing shapeshifter killed Clamella.'

There was another loud splash. 'I'm still here you know,' said Pearl.

'Yes, of course. This is, unfortunately, the latest in a string of fae murders which we believe to have been committed by the same er... shapeshifter. But naturally, because he keeps changing what he looks like, it will be difficult for us to apprehend him immediately.' Ned scratched his head. 'Especially when the main facts of the other cases have been withheld.'

Pearl looked confused. 'But you know who it is now, can't you just...' She made a swiping gesture with her arms. 'You know, go get him?'

Ned was trying to think of an explanation as to why they couldn't exactly just *go get him* when another thought occurred to him. 'Why do you need us to catch him if you already know who killed Clamella?'

Pearl scowled. 'He left the water before we found her body.'

'But 'ow do you know that?' asked Jenni.

Pearl rolled her eyes. 'Because, all merpeople have a unique sonar signal and we can ping each other's location. We obviously did a tail count when we discovered the murder and his tail was missing. We could not find him.'

Jenni was impressed. 'Bet that's 'andy though.'

'Not when the murderous son of a lagos tries to hide himself on land.' She pressed a hand to her forehead, scrunching her eyes as she focused the sonar. It didn't take long. Her eyes snapped open and Pearl pointed behind Ned. 'I've found him. He's in there.'

# Chapter 12

Ned inspected the plain wooden building that stood on the pier. It had one door and window that he could see, and it most definitely hadn't been there yesterday. Peering closer he saw a poker chip rotating in the window.

'Is that...?'

'Yep.' Jenni answered before Ned had time to finish the question.

'You have to go in and apprehend the murderer!' pleaded Pearl.

'Why don't you go?' demanded Jenni.

'Uh, hello!' The mermaid splashed her tail down hard and a wave of water hit the pier.

'Just cos you haven't got legs...' muttered Jenni but stopped when Ned glared at her.

'I'm sorry, but we can't go in and get him, Pearl. That poker game is buy-in only. Ten thousand gold bits.' Ned looked at the building wistfully. 'We'll have to wait for the game to finish and the players to come out.'

'But why can't you go in? Surely land law extends to some shack. It's right there.' Pearl was confused.

'It ain't that simple. The doorway is keyed to your buy-in, see. If you don't 'ave the coins then you can't get in,' explained Jenni. 'It's a magically constructed building, so what 'appens inside, stays inside.' She looked up at Ned. 'There's magical safeguards and stuff, to protect the players. And no-one leaves 'til there's a winner.'

'You seem to know a lot about it, Jenni.'

'Well, I fawt it were important to find out 'sidering catchers ain't allowed and wotnot,' she replied, thinking fast and doing her best innocent face.

'Yes, well, I suppose a good thief-catcher does needs to know all about what they shouldn't be doing.' He turned his attention back to the mermaid. 'Unfortunately, Pearl, the Emperor has forbidden participation in the poker tournament by any member of law enforcement. So, there's no way I could go in and get him. But we can wait for Armando to come out when the tournament is over.'

'If 'e comes out. No telling wot might 'appen, 'e might slip out the back or summik,' commented Jenni.

Ned glared at her, but she grinned back, unconcerned, and carried on talking.

'Anyways, Boss - dontcha have some 'oliday to take? Very 'laxing, poker is.'

'No!' Pearl interrupted. 'That's not good enough! Are we not citizens of Roshaven?' She lashed her tail in the water angrily and the beauty glamour she'd been projecting began to slip revealing wicked looking talons, razor sharp spikes on her tail, and a mouth full of fanged teeth. 'Call yourself a thief-catcher? You couldn't catch a starfish!' She lunged for his foot, which still dangled over the edge of the pier, but was repelled by an invisible barrier. Ned patted the remains of the amulet that still hung around his neck in wonder before Jenni coughed pointedly. The tips of Ned's ears turned red.

'Pearl, calm down, please,' he said. 'It's not that I don't want to help you, I do. But I simply can't walk in there empty-handed. They wouldn't let me in the hut without the gold buy-in and if I did go in, it sounds like I'd have to play poker and wait for end of the tournament before I could arrest him.'

Pearl's eyes narrowed to thin slits. She abruptly dove beneath the surface. Ned took the opportunity to hastily put his last sock and boot back onto his foot and scramble away from the edge of the pier. He was just in time as a barnacle encrusted chest flew out of the water and landed millimetres from his feet.

'Will that do?' asked Pearl reappearing, beautiful again and seemingly a little more under control.

Ned warily opened the lid of the chest, let it close, then opened it again. It was full of gold coins, easily worth ten thousand gold bits.

'I can't take this...' he began.

'We want you to apprehend Clamella's murderer. You need gold; here is gold,' replied Pearl.

'No, I mean, I literally can't lift it.' Ned said as he nudged the heavy chest with his boot. It didn't budge.

'Surely your sprite can do something?' Pearl waved a hand at Jenni who was being unusually quiet. 'You must hurry, the tournament entry closes at midday. I don't think they'll let you in if you're late.'

Ned turned to look at the small building again. Sure enough, a clock hung on the door. It was still ticking, but the hour hand had reached the number twelve with the minute hand not far behind.

'Please!' implored Pearl.

Ned felt helpless to resist, and it wasn't only her fishy charms. A murder was a murder was a murder. He turned purposefully and strode towards the building. 'Jenni, lighten the chest. We're going in.' He faltered when he realised Jenni wasn't following him. 'Jenni?'

She was looking down, kicking the bone deck with her left foot, trying to find the right words.

'Jenni? What is it?' asked Ned.

'Boss,' she said in a small voice. 'I ain't sure this is a

good idea, Boss. I mean, do you really fink this is the best use of Catcher resources?' Momma K's warning was giving her second, third and fourth thoughts now that it looked like Ned would be able to enter the game.

'We're thief-catchers, Jenni.' Ned was bemused. 'We solve crimes, we catch bad guys and there's one in that hut, right now. We have to go in, before we run out of time.'

Jenni eyed the clock. 'The fing is, Boss... the fing is... right, what it is, is... er, I mean, it's wotsit right? Ain't good for you. Gambling and all that. Mebbe we could go in and not play. Cos of the Emperor's decree an' all.' She warmed to her topic, thinking if could convince him to go in but not play, she'd get around Momma K's orders. 'The Emperor innit it. He said, didn't he? Anyone wot went in was against the laws, right and youse meant to keep the laws so you can't. So, go in, yeah and keep an eye on it all then catch 'im.' She sniffed loudly. 'And anyways if you win you don't get the money. Plus, you ain't gonna win. So... no point really is there?' She beamed at him, pleased with her logic. Pearl looked on in consternation.

'Since when have you ever walked away from a challenge, Jenni? We've got the opportunity to get in there and catch this murderous metamorph. Come on, sort out the chest. Please. Now.'

'But Boss, just cos you've got the gold bits don't mean you're gonna get 'im. Going frew there means you gotta play and you ain't no good at poker.'

Ned ignored her, marched up to the door and began to open it just as the minute hand touched on twelve.

Muttering under her breath Jenni lightened the chest and sent it floating in after Ned before stomping in after them. The door shut with a bang and then fizzed gently as the magical lock-in coalesced into being.

# Chapter 13

Ned's eyes took a moment to adjust to the dim, smoky atmosphere. It was odd because no one was actually smoking. The smoke had been invited for the ambience and it was doing a great job. A large oval table with six chairs around it dominated the room. There was a tank of water at the head of the table and a seventh chair from a neglected pile in the corner was being rapidly dusted and shuffled into position.

'Jenni? How will we know who the shapeshifter is?' Ned asked as they stood at the threshold.

Jenni's gaze darted left and right. 'The fing is, Boss. I ain't not meant to be 'ere.'

'What do you mean?'

'Miss Jenni, we need you!' called a voice from the far side of the room.

'Look, Boss. I'm the muscle and I didn't tell you cos fing.' She paused and shrugged. 'I knew it were wrong, but Momma K wanted me 'ere. So, it is wot it is.' She started walking away then stopped and turned back to face Ned. 'Silver eyes. 'E ain't gonna be able to shift in 'ere. But 'is eyes'll be silver. Good luck, Boss.'

Ned watched his second-in-command walk away and tried not to feel snippy. He failed. Silver eyes was something Jenni could've shared with him at the beginning of the murder investigations. And as for working the tournament, he'd heard the whole team talk about what they'd each do if they'd won the money. Reg had even been thinking of setting up a regular poker night down in The Noose. And throughout all the discussions, Jenni had known she was going to be here. Watching the game hand by hand and she hadn't even offered to get Ned in as a spectator.

He looked around the room. There was a young girl behind the bar on the other side of the hut talking to a lad dressed as a waiter. Clustered near the poker table stood the other players. Behind the transparent wall to his left there were rows of seats being gradually filled by the citizens of Roshaven. He took a hesitant step further into the room and stopped when his attention was caught by something frantically moving. It was Fred waving madly at him. Ned nodded towards the young palace guard and managed a half smile. *Great*, he thought, *not only am I playing a game I barely know the rules to, but I'm being watched by half the city.*

'I'll take that, Sir.' It was the voice who had called Jenni over. Or rather, it was the body the voice belonged to.

'Jimmy Fingers? What are you doing here?'

The young man flushed and dropped the posh act. 'Yeah, alright Spinks. Working, en't I. How you doing?'

'Been better.'

'I heard. Mermaids got you into a right pickle, ain't they?' Fingers was grinning.

'How did you know about that?'

'We were all watching you out on the pier.'

The tips of Ned's ears turned red.

'Not much to do while we waited for the game to begin but everyone's here now.' Fingers pointed at the chest. 'I'll need to take that.'

'Feel free.'

Fingers nodded his thanks and started dragging the chest towards a pile of wealth in the far corner, guarded by a dragon.

*Risky choice,* thought Ned, *dragons are a law unto themselves.* When the dragon winked at Ned, he realised it was a magical illusion, probably hiding some kind of deadly attack if anyone tried to steal the gold. The giveaway was the wink. Dragons never wink. Obviously, Momma K had left nothing to chance. If it looked like a dragon was protecting the gold coin, in theory, the run of the mill thief would think twice. Ned could feel a tightness over his skin. That would be the magical forcefields preventing non-players from entering the room and probably a general dampener field preventing any magic usage. He tried a simple power grab. Nothing happened. That didn't necessarily mean anything, six times out of ten nothing happened but this felt different. It felt like something rubbery was in his way. Ned felt discombobulated. At least that's what he thought he was feeling. *Get a grip, Spinks,* he told himself. *You can do this. It's only a game of cards.*

'Awright everyone, gather round.' Jenni called out. The seven players came to the table. Ned risked half a smile when he saw the octopus from his office sitting in the tank in the dealer's spot, its tentacles draping over the edge. The octopus waved one tentacle in greeting then expertly shuffled a deck of cards.

'Okay, so 'ere it is. You've all stumped up ten fousand bits to be in this game, right? The 'ouse takes its ten percent entry fee for starters and we gives you lot jools to play wiv. Grand winner keeps all jools and rest of the gold.' She looked around the room, making sure there were no objections. 'K. Gerald 'ere is your dealer. E's aufentick so don't worry 'bout that. Fingers'll get you a drink or whatever from the bar if you wants it. No loo breaks, no leaving the table without forfeit, no canoodling.' There was nervous laughter. 'We're playin'

Texas 'Old 'Em and Gerald will tell you wot your blinds is. Any questions?'

'Can we sit where we like?' asked one of the players.

'Yeah, 'course. It ain't school,' Jenni replied.

There was a scramble to the table. Ned ended up opposite a fat man dressed in white, a trilby on his head, a neat black goatee around his jowls and most conspicuously, an immaculately kept moustache. The man tipped his hat at Ned and winked, the light catching his silvery eyes. It was the shapeshifter. Armando.

To Ned's right was a female dwarf. He could tell she was female despite the carefully groomed beard, most dwarfs were very proud of their facial growth. It was the stench of highly perfumed roses that gave her away. Jenni was performing a weapon shake down, divesting the dwarf of various axes and throwing knives. The flurry of the shake down wafted the perfume again and again. Beyond the dwarf sat the cephalopod dealer, Gerald. On his right was Mr. Simms, the undead psychiatrist who specialised in grief counselling and couples' therapy. There was something about his positive mental attitude that helped those who'd recently lost loved ones believe their dead were in a better place and his happy-go-lucky attitude to having outlived his last four wives that made him an excellent sounding board for couples in trouble.

On Ned's left sat a wood nymph. Ned thanked his lucky stars for Willow's charm bracelet. Having her on the thief-catcher team had been touch and go to start with thanks to Willow's naturally high levels of pheromones and inability to stop sexually attracting the other catchers. A simple bracelet of her hair made Ned immune. But it looked like Momma K's magical dampening was restricting everyone's natural abilities, and not just Ned's meagre spellcaster power, because the nymph looked almost normal. If you ignored the well-placed ivy leaves and smooth nut-brown skin.

Beyond her was a water sprite. Again, Momma K's restrictions had forced the sprite to choose one form and so a translucent humanoid shape sloshed quietly in the chair. It was difficult to make out actual facial features as the water sprite had neglected to project eyes, nose, or mouth but Ned supposed it must be able to communicate somehow otherwise it wouldn't be there. He did wonder briefly how a nymph or a water sprite, who had no need for money on a day to day basis, could afford the ten thousand gold bits buy-in price but then he supposed immortal elementals had ample time to accumulate much more than that over the years. A second question followed the first - why then were they playing poker? Ned had no idea. As long as they didn't make him look too terrible. All he wanted was to get through the game with most of his credibility intact so he could arrest Armando as soon as the tournament was finished. He risked another glance at the shapeshifter. He was busy talking to the gnome on his right, completely ignoring Mr. Simms to his left.

Gnomes are often confused with dwarfs, especially in the beard growing department, however, they tended to be squatter. Both species had a genuine love for gold, axes, being underground, and quaffing. It went with the beard territory. However, call a gnome a dwarf, or vice versa, and you were likely to lose your kneecaps. They were fiercely protective of their individual identities. The fact that no one else could tell them apart didn't matter. Ned had had plenty of practice in the riots on Teacake Alley when a series of inflammatory comments – gnomes claiming dwarves were too short to dig for gold while dwarves claimed gnomes couldn't grow a decent beard to save their lives - had blown apart the uneasy peace the two species usually held.

'Boss? Arms up, please.' It was Jenni, ready to check him for weapons. Ned complied without thinking and reddened when Jenni took away three knives, a set of knuckle dusters, and a vial of poison. It made him look a lot more badass than he actually was. The vial didn't even belong to him, it was evidence in another case that he'd forgotten to enter. He tried to make a mental note, but his nerves unsettled him.

'Afore you get your jools, let's have a quick whizz round wiv names, yeah?' Jenni nodded encouragingly at the dwarf to begin.

'Ignaceta.' She looked expectantly at Ned.

'Er, Ned Spinks.'

'Ivy,' purred the nymph.

'Gurgle gurgle gurgle,' went the sprite. No one seemed bothered apart from Ned who felt sure that wasn't its name.

'Volcanite.' The gnome lifted its chin, daring anyone to comment on the similarity in names with the dwarf but no one felt like risking a knee.

'Armando, at your service.' The shapeshifter kept his eyes on Ned as he spoke.

'And I am Mr. Simms.' The zombie shrink beamed at everyone.

'Great. Play fair, I'll be watching. Good luck!' Jenni clapped her hands. A pile of jewels appeared in front of each player. Everyone had four pearls, three emeralds, two sapphires, two diamonds, three rubies and two large, gold bars. Ned swallowed. There was more wealth on the table directly in front of him then he'd ever earnt. One of the precious stones could set him up for life. A vague notion of winning tickled the back of his mind, but he pushed it away and risked a glance at Armando, who was grinning back at him.

Gerald the octopus dealt each player two cards then held up a pearl, and an emerald to indicate the blinds, and gestured towards the dwarf to begin the play. The first round began gently. Everyone checked to begin with, and the octopus dealt the jack of hearts, the two of diamonds and the three of spades. This led to a flurry of surreptitious card looking as nervous players couldn't remember what they had. The nymph braved the first bet, rolling a pearl into the centre of the table, causing the gnome, Mr. Simms and the dwarf to fold. The rest of the players matched the bet. Gerald tried to calm the palpable nerves in the room with some encouraging tentacling before dealing the four of diamonds. No one bet until Armando flicked an emerald into the centre of the table.

Jenni was standing at Ned's elbow. 'He finks no one's got nuffink. Trying to get you all to fold. 'E's buying the pot the cheeky sod,' she muttered.

Ned was grateful for the commentary, it helped keep his nerves under control. Both he and Ivy matched the bet whilst the water sprite folded. The octopus dealt the seven of clubs and Ned stayed his hand, but Ivy was glaring daggers at Armando and added a pearl to the pot. He grinned, matching her and raising another emerald.

Ned wanted to roll his eyes at the posturing, instead, he matched the bet, as did Ivy. A reveal of cards gave Armando a low straight and he collected his winnings gleefully.

Ned was parched. He felt like he'd run for miles and yet they'd only played one round. It might look calm and collected on the surface, but the tension was palpable and everyone, bar Armando, was showing their nerves one way or another. There was a lot of finger tapping, hair twirling, coughing, shifting, nose rubbing, and jewel fiddling. Jenni's eyes were swivelling all over the place as she tried to sort out the nerves from any cheating, but everyone was too jittery for her to tell. She motioned to Fingers to take a pass at the table for a drinks order. This piece of normality calmed the players somewhat and they went into the next round.

# Chapter 14

Everyone seemed reluctant to start the betting until it was Armando's turn. He threw a pearl into the centre causing Ignaceta to fling her cards down in disgust and fold. She tutted loudly as Ned checked his cards. The noise made him flinch and he dropped one of his cards on the table, picture side up, revealing a ten of clubs. Feeling flustered, he tried to cover his embarrassment by matching the bet. Ivy folded with a smile and the octopus dealt the two of clubs, the three of spades and the two of diamonds.

Ned looked around the table, wondering why no one was doing anything. Jenni poked him in the back and whispered. Loudly. 'It's you. In or out, Boss?'

'Oh, right. Er...' Embarrassed, Ned looked at his cards and then at his jewels. He thought he might have something, but he'd run out of pearls. He gestured beseechingly at Gerald who nodded and let him put in an emerald, taking out four pearls. There was a fair bit of grumbling from the other players around the table until the octopus banged loudly on his glass and waved the deck of cards around.

'E's right, wot the dealer says goes. If you don't like it, you can leave.' Jenni glared at the players, daring someone to quit. No one did. The water sprite folded, and Gerald dealt the nine of spades. Knowing he didn't really have anything and feeling like he'd risked enough already this hand, Ned folded too. He took a beer from Fingers gratefully and spent the rest of the play sipping his beverage, trying to steady his nerves. The round ended with the gnome going head to head with Armando but, yet again, the shapeshifter won the hand much to the general dislike from the rest of the table.

Round three and after getting their cards, all the players checked. Ned was managing to stay relatively calm until Gerald dealt the queen of diamonds, the king of clubs and the king of hearts. There was a collective *oooooh* from the spectators beyond the glass making Ned start in surprise. He had forgotten about the audience. The cards on the table seemed to encourage the players and the blinds were quickly bet. Then Armando threw a sapphire in.

'Mmm, stakes could be a bit 'igh on this one, Boss. Everyone's a bit nervy.' Jenni was back at Ned's shoulder. He was grateful for her presence as Gerald dealt the nine of spades. There was a cascade of folding leaving the water sprite, Ned and Armando in the hand. The seven of spades followed.

Ned looked at his cards again. Then glanced at the ones on the table. He had a king and a seven. He had this round. Trying hard not to show his excitement, Ned matched Armando's sapphire and added a ruby.

'Easy, Boss,' Jenni warned him as first the water sprite matched the bet then Armando followed. The shapeshifter continued to grin at Ned and started playing with his pearls. The cards were revealed. The sprite had a pair of nines and a pair of kings. He gurgled happily. Armando's grin faltered as he revealed a pair of sevens and a pair of kings. He downed his drink, slamming the empty glass on the table and imperiously waving Fingers over for a refill. The sprite burbled in delight and turned to face Ned, at least Ned thought he did. Slowly, Ned turned over his cards revealing three kings and two sevens. A full house. The sprite sagged a little, turning more ovoid than humanoid. Ned reached into the middle of the table to collect his winnings.

A little electric thrill ran through his body as he considered the possibility that he could win this. His brain started surging forwards with all the things he could do with the money. He could buy new boots. He could get a secretary to do all his paperwork. He could take a holiday.

A loud sloshing noise returned Ned's attention to the table. The dealer had already dealt the next hand and the sprite was burbling joyfully. At least, Ned thought he was. The dwarf folded in disgust, again, as everyone else placed a pearl bet and Gerald dealt the five of spades, jack of diamonds and the nine of diamonds.

'It's a nuffink 'and, Boss. Play it steady.' Jenni was back in his ear, cautioning Ned. He and everyone else risked nothing more than a pearl except for Ivy who folded with a two of spades and the ace of diamonds.

When Gerald dealt the ace of spades, the nymph bursts into tears at the loss of what could have been a winning hand. Jenni moved past Ned and whispered comforting things in her ear. Emotions were running high as more pearls were rolled into the centre of the table. Cautious betting so far. Gerald added the three of hearts as the gnome checked, revealing he had nothing. Armando was grinning again. He picked up an emerald and looked around the table. Then he changed his mind and threw a sapphire into the centre. The watching audience gasped. Fingers, always the entrepreneur, was hawking fresh popcorn, doing a roaring trade. Mr. Simms matched the bet and looked dead-eyed at Ned. He couldn't help it; it was just the way his eyes were. Ned swallow nervously, there wasn't much in the hand. Armando was still grinning. Wishing he could wipe the smile off that fat face, Ned reluctantly put a sapphire into the game. With everyone else folded, Armando and Mr. Simms matched the raise and the three of them revealed their cards.

Armando had two nines, trumped easily by Mr. Simms with two Ace's and leaving Ned trailing behind with two jacks.

'Never mind, Boss. It's still anyone's game,' Jenni piped up encouragingly. 'And anyways you ain't playing to win, are you? Just to get 'im at the end.' She tipped her head towards Armando.

Ned nodded slowly. He was only there to make sure the shapeshifter didn't escape from justice. That's all. He had absolutely no stake in this game whatsoever. *So why are my palms feeling so clammy and my stomach is in knots?* he thought.

Going into the fifth round, by some unspoken agreement, some of the players upped the ante and began betting with emeralds instead of pearls. Mostly because Armando had won a large proportion of the pearls, but also because there was an air of determination about the table. A sense of getting on with the game. However, the water sprite and the gnome folded before Gerald dealt his three cards - the two of spades, seven of spades and six of spades. The rest of the players went still and the general hubbub of conversation from the audience went quiet. This could be a major hand.

Armando chuckled at the two players who'd folded. 'Bet you wish you hadn't done that,' he gloated.

'They're all panicking, Boss.' Jenni was back. 'Could be a flush, see. You gotta bluff this one out. S'all for the taking now.'

Armando clanged a gold bar onto the table. It was swiftly followed by one from Ignaceta but Ned dithered.

He had a spade in his hand so was on for a flush but then anyone else could be as well. And it was a gold bar bet. That felt like a big step up. The game was feeling more serious now, more personal, which was ridiculous. The gold bar wasn't even his.

'Any time, Boss.' Jenni waggled her eyebrows at him, and Ned reluctantly put the bar into the centre of the table. Ivy matched them and Gerald dealt the two of hearts. There was muttering from the audience and the other players held their breath, waiting to see what Armando would do.

He twirled a diamond into the centre of the table.

'You got no choice, Boss. You can't give in now.' Jenni whispered in his ear. It seemed as if the rest of the table heard her and three more diamonds followed. Every single eyeball watched the dealing tentacle as it revealed the nine of spades.

Grinning, as always, Armando added in another gold bar. Not to be outdone, Ignaceta matched and raised with a ruby. Throwing caution to the wind Ned and Ivy added to the pile. Ned especially tried not to think about the value of the huge pile of gems on the table in front of him. It didn't work and he watched with rising panic as Armando added in the ruby, looked at the additional gems he'd acquired in front of him and pushed in four emeralds. He looked craftily around the room and added another four.

'That's not fair!' yelled Ignaceta, her beard bristling. 'We don't have that many emeralds available.'

'Looks like I'm getting a new diamond watch,' replied Armando, turning to look at the dealer who was in consultation with Jenni.

'Right, this is wot it is. You can swap in diamonds for either a sapphy or an emerald.' She rounded on

Armando. 'And you can stop being a cocky sod an' all.'

He grinned toothily at her, silver eyes flashing in the light.

Once the players had added in their jewels, it was time to show the hands. Armando revealed the ace of spades. He'd won with a high flush and everyone knew it as they turned their own cards over in stony silence. The shapeshifter didn't care, he leaned forwards and slowly hauled back his winnings.

Jenni read the room and clapped her hands together loudly. 'We're having five minutes. Loo break, smoke break, whatever.' She pressed a button on the side of the table and a pre-made magical stasis field was activated. It covered the game, protecting each player's stack and preventing any pilfering.

Everyone except Armando seemed glad of the break. The shapeshifter seemed a little annoyed at having his winning streak interrupted, so he went to the bar to console himself.

'Boss? Sploshy wants a word.' Jenni snagged Ned's attention and motioned him over to where the water sprite stood.

'Gurgle, gurgle, gurgle?' asked the water sprite.

Ned smiled and nodded slowly then looked at Jenni for a translation.

'E wants to know wot the mermaids wanted wiv you. I'll tell him, Boss. I don't fink you've got the liquid.' Jenni splashed, sloshed and splished in response before turning back to Ned. 'I told 'im 'bout the murder and the kiniving shifter wot done it.' She glared at Armando's back.

'Jenni?' Ned was watching the water sprite who was literally boiling with rage.

'Yeah?' She turned back and yelped at the bubbling,

steaming column of water. 'Calm down mate! Wot's up?'

The water sprite hissed and spat in response. Ned took a slight side-step. He'd already had his dunking for the day. Eventually, the sprite stopped communicating and calmed down to a simmer.

'Boss, 'e's done a novver water fae. Same as the mermaids and the nixies. 'E went to the water sprites 'ome, ingratiated 'imself. Learning 'ow to ebb and flow and such like. Then, as they were all trusting 'im and every fink, 'e wiped out their source well. Every single one of 'em dissolved. Like that!' She slapped her hands together sharply.

Unable to process that much casual destruction, Ned asked the obvious question. 'Why wasn't, er Gurgle, destroyed as well?'

'I dunno,' she turned to the sprite. 'Well?'

There was more sploshing but this time it was self-pitying with fewer ripples.

'Right, funny fing, Boss. 'E was visiting the mermaids when it 'appened. They caught the resonance in the water and was able to deflect it. Patch it up wiv a little o' their own. There's a bit o' salt in 'is soul now.' She stopped talking as Armando passed them.

Pausing, he looked directly at the water sprite. 'You're looking a little dry,' he commented.

The sprite lunged for the shapeshifter but was repelled by a magical shield that shimmered into existence.

'No violence,' Jenni said unhappily.

The rest of the players returned to the table. The water sprite gathered his remaining jewels, glared at Armando, and defiantly placed them in front of Ned. The shapeshifter opened his mouth to protest but stopped when he realised no one else was speaking. In fact,

everyone was deadly silent, even the audience beyond
the partition.

# Chapter 15

With everyone sitting down, Jenni went to stand next to the octopus' tank and waited for Gerald to begin. This time one tentacle held up an emerald, while another held up a sapphire. The blinds had gone up.

Settling into the game, all the players checked. The previous betting frenzy had calmed down and after Gerald dealt the six of hearts, seven of diamonds and king of hearts, only pearls were bet. Even that was too much for Ivy and Volcanite and they both folded. A queen of diamonds was dealt. Armando checked; the others added a pearl.

Ned felt uneasy. Up to this point, the shapeshifter had been betting aggressively, now Armando was playing it way too safe. It didn't track. Something was going on. Emboldened, Ned raised the pot with a ruby forcing the other players to follow suit.

The final card was dealt, the nine of diamonds. Again, Armando checked. It seemed to have a bizarre effect on the other players as Mr. Simms raised with an emerald and Iganceta astounded everyone by going all in. There were faint cries of *You're crazy* and *What are you doing?* from the audience beyond the poker room. Ned looked at Ignaceta sideways. Did she really have that good a hand? Or was this all some weird plot. For what, he didn't know. The table was too rich for him; he needed to be sensible and fold. He didn't have anything anyway, just another queen to make a pair. He wasn't going to win with a pair of queens.

'Can't handle the pressure eh, Spinks?' Armando

finally addressed Ned directly. 'You haven't got the stones to sit at the big boy table. Give in. Walk away. You aren't going to win anyway.'

Ned could feel his ears reddening. It was true, he didn't have the experience to be sitting at such a prestigious poker game, but he was here and it was damned if he was going to let some silver-eyed, murderous, son of shifter tell him what he could and couldn't do! Ned realised he was breathing hard and his hands shook slightly as he matched the pot with a pearl, two emeralds, three sapphires and a ruby. His sensible voice was screaming in the back of his head, but he'd become quite good at ignoring that one.

Armando chortled to himself as he too joined the bet then immediately turned over his cards as Mr. Simms was adding his jewels to the centre. He had nothing, the ace of hearts and the seven of clubs. Ned gaped at him in surprise. Mr. Simms was muttering as he also lost the hand but Ignaceta looked like the dwarf who'd got the gold seam as she collected her winnings.

'You can't let 'im get in yor 'ead, Boss,' scolded Jenni. 'It don't matter to 'im wot the cards are. 'E's playing the pot, trying to get youse lot to lose your jools. Watch yourself, Boss. Don't get too vested.'

Ned knew she was right. It had been a dirty trick, and he was more annoyed with himself for giving into the goading than for the jewels he'd lost. There was a low hubbub from the crowd as the players placed the blinds and Gerald dealt their cards.

'Keep an ear out, Boss. I fink we've got some cheatin' going on.' Jenni whispered in Ned's ear then sauntered off, leering at each player individually as she passed. Naturally, everyone had heard her comment, and so those that were guilty of cheating looked nervous and those that weren't cheating but were worried they'd be accused also looked nervous.

Ned and Ivy picked up their cards at the same time, both making small snorts as they saw what they had. Realising they were echoing each other, Ivy pulled her cards closer, eyeing Ned with suspicion. *At least I know I'm not cheating*, thought Ned glumly as both Mr. Simms and Volcanite coughed at the same time then glared at each other. Jenni was trying to look everywhere at once and doing a pretty decent job.

With every player on edge, they all checked, even Armando. Gerald dealt the nine of spades, the king of spades, and the two of spades. There was groaning from the audience. Ned felt his stomach sink. It was another spades round. That had gone so well last time.

Volcanite started playing with a pearl in his left hand while Mr. Simms checked. Armando did nothing, yet Ignaceta tapped the table once and put an emerald into the middle. Ned watched with amusement as the other players tried to decide whether these tics had been there all the time and they hadn't noticed or whether some of them were actually cheating. He folded with clubs; he was staying well out of this round. Ivy rubbed her nose excessively before adding an emerald, causing both Volcanite and Ignaceta to frown at each other. Ned wondered whether there was more than one arrangement among the players at the table. Could the nymph be working with both the gnome and the dwarf? It was, after all, an interspecies poker game.

Volcanite put pay to Ned's speculation by folding. *Unless of course he'd been signalled to do so* mused Ned, trying to see if anyone looked particularly pleased. Most of the other players were concentrating on the game, but Armando, of course, was grinning as he tossed an emerald into bet. Mr. Simms matched him almost immediately and turned expectantly to the dealer. The four of hearts appeared.

'Some bold cards there, Boss. Look at Ivy, she's low on jools. Watch 'em circle 'er. You're well out of this one, Boss.' This time Jenni did manage to whisper. In fact, she was so quiet, Ned could barely hear her at all. But a quick glance proved that Ivy was indeed running low on gems and this would be a good opportunity to get rid of her as a player. If your cards were better than hers, of course. Ignaceta raised the pot with a ruby and after much agonising over her reduced wealth, Ivy followed. Armando rubbed his hands and eyed the huge pile of jewels in front of him. He looked over at Ivy and seemed to mentally tot up what she had left. Then he raised the pot with the exact number of gems she had.

'Evil git,' muttered Jenni, but Ned looked over at the shapeshifter's pile. He could've easily bet a lot more than he did. It was a clear message - I'm coming for you.

Ivy's ivy was trembling as she clutched her cards watching to see what would happen next. Mr. Simms tutted as he folded. Ignaceta matched the wager reluctantly. The betting was beginning to get out of hand. Ivy swallowed as the octopus extended a tentacle in her direction. She went all in. Gerald dealt the six of diamonds.

The players at the table watched expectantly. Not a soul in the audience moved a muscle. Everyone waited to see what Armando would do. He checked and Ignaceta copied, blowing her cheeks out in relief that she hadn't lost any more jewels. She looked at Volcanite as she revealed an eight of spades and ten of hearts. She had nothing. Volcanite shook his head in commiseration.

Ivy looked at Armando defiantly, tipping her chin to

him, offering him the opportunity to go first. He revealed three kings. She let the cards in her hand tumble to the table. Jenni nipped in and turned them gently over. A pair of fours and a pair of nines.

As Ivy woodenly got up from the table, Armando tipped his hat at her.

'Bye-bye, little tree. Too bad, so sad,' he said whilst grinning his insufferable grin, oblivious to the entire table looking daggers at him. He imperiously ordered another drink from Fingers. No one except Ned noticed but, Fingers spat in the drink at the bar and the barmaid stirred it in well.

Despite the kerfuffle, Gerald gestured for the game to continue with a loud rap of one of his tentacles on the side of his tank. He dealt the next round of cards.

Ignaceta fiddled with an emerald, looked at Ned then put it back and placed her bet with a pearl. The other players followed. Armando didn't even bother to look at his cards.

The octopus dealt the four of spades, the nine of clubs and the six of hearts. On seeing the cards, Ignaceta ran her forefinger under her chin. Volcanite copied her exactly. Jenni was watching with narrowed eyes. Ignaceta checked.

Ned leaned forward, debating what to bet, when Jenni interrupted his thought process by slapping a hand on top of his cards, making him jump.

'Oi, 'ang on a minute. Youse two is copying each uvver or summik. Wot's going on?' She glared at the dwarf and gnome. 'Tell me the truth,' she took a small glass bottle out of her pocket and broke it on the floor as she spoke. Glittering blue smoke wreathed its way around both players. It was another previously prepared spell.

'No! You can't...' Ignaceta started to yell but the magic took over and she stopped protesting. 'Yes, I am working with the gnome.'

Volcanite had been avoiding the smoke by refusing to breathe but at Ignaceta's reveal he let out a hah of irritation. Instantly cowed by the truth smoke he nodded, glassy-eyed.

'Yes, the dwarf and I were going to split the winnings. Don't tell my clan leader.' The request was made without feeling thanks to the spell, but several dwarfs and gnomes banged angrily on the spectator glass.

Jenni puffed her chest out in pride at having caught the cheating culprits. She herded the dwarf and the gnome over to the door and gave a complicated knock. The door unfastened and Jenni proceeded to kick the two unresisting players out of the hut. The arc of their ejection was trailed by the sparkly blue truth smoke. The audience dwarves and gnomes were competing to get out of the spectator seating first in order to harangue their failed players for having been caught.

'They ain't being allowed to play again,' Jenni said in satisfaction as the door closed. She looked around the table at the remaining players. 'Let that be a lesson to you - if yor gonna cheat, don't get caught!' She leaned into the table and pushed the jewels that belonged to Volcanite into the middle. Then walked round and did the same to Ignaceta's. The pot was now ridiculously wealthy.

Ned felt sick. 'I don't have to match that, do I?'

Gerald explained, via Jenni.

'S'alright, Boss. This 'and is void now, see? But the jools will stay there and be added to the winner of the next one.' She gave him an encouraging wink. 'Never know, Boss. Could be you.'

Gerald held up a ruby and a diamond to indicate that the blinds were going up again. Ned swallowed, it seemed they were getting to the serious end of the game. The remaining players all bet a diamond. Ned looked at the three cards on the table. The queen of diamonds, the eight of diamonds and the two of diamonds. Trying hard to quash his rising excitement, Ned risked a glance at the other players. Mr. Simms, being dead, was hard to read at the best of times but was that a slight bloom of colour on his pallid skin? Armando was grinning, even wider than usual.

Ned decided to take it as a good sign and nervously pushed a gold bar into the centre of the table. Armando matched and raised it instantly with another one. The two men stared at each other. Both of them thinking that this was it, this was the hand to play for.

Mr. Simms coughed, 'I am still playing, you know,' he said but no one paid any attention. They were all focused on the staring match. Huffily Mr. Simms banged two gold bars onto the table. Ned did nothing.

'Boss! You've gotta raise a bar to stay in.' Jenni told Ned helpfully.

Without breaking his gaze, Ned fumbled around the table looking for the gold bars. Jenni tutted and guided his hand. He tossed it into the centre where it knocked over the existing stack with a clang.

Gerald dealt the queen of hearts. Ned could feel his pulse quickening, he had two queens and now there were two on the table. This was his hand. Ned narrowed his eyes at Armando, trying to psyche the shapeshifter out. Faking confidence, Ned pushed in three rubies, another diamond and three pearls.

Armando matched without pause, grinning. Then he

very purposefully broke their staring contest and looked at Mr. Simms who was sitting next to him. He craned his neck slightly, mentally counting all the gems the zombie had left in front of him. He raised the exact amount.

Mr. Simms, delighted at finally being taken notice of, laughed, shrugged and went all in. He accepted the shapeshifters challenge, confident in his hand. Ned felt a flicker of nerves as every eyeball in the place swivelled to watch what he would do. He went for it. You could've heard a pin drop. Jenni sneezed, loudly, making Ned jump.

Gerald dealt the ace of spades and tentacled Armando to show his cards first. He revealed a pair of eights and a pair of queens.

Mr. Simms let out a triumphant 'Hah!' and showed a flush of diamonds. Armando shrugged, trying to conceal his surprise at having his hand beaten, his overconfidence having finally got the better of him. Ned turned his own cards over to display the four queens of the pack however Mr. Simms thought he'd still won and was leaning over to gather in the huge pile of jewels towards him.

'Ah ah ah dead-boy, you ain't won. Four queens trump a flush mate, even if you 'ave got all diamonds,' said Jenni, delighted for her boss.

Mr. Simms sagged and turned a definite paler shade of grey. Jenni led him away from the table gently. Ned looked on in disbelief. He had also thought that a flush beat a two-pair. He made no move to collect his winnings, so Gerald rolled his eyes and leant over the side of his tank to push the winnings Ned's way.

'Just you and me now, thief-catcher. Looks like you've finally got the gems to go up against me.' Armando stroked his moustache in satisfaction.

'I don't care about the game,' bluffed Ned, unconvincingly. 'Soon as this is over, I'm going to arrest you for a string of fae murders.'

Armando chortled making Ned angry. Before he could let loose a string of expletives he'd been collecting at the murderous shapeshifter, Armando spoke again.

'Let's raise the stakes. If I win, I walk away with the jewels and the money. And if I lose,' he paused for effect, milking the moment but went on for too long and the crowd starting yelling for him to get on with it. 'If I lose, you can arrest me. I won't shift.'

'Is that a confession?'

Armando ran two fingers over his moustache and said nothing.

'What about the fact that I'm already winning?' asked Ned.

Armando shrugged. 'It's a fluke, nothing else. Did you really think you were good enough to play against me?' He gestured at the empty seats. 'I got rid of the others. I can beat you. Do we have a deal?'

Throughout the game the shapeshifter had been getting under Ned's skin with his smug attitude and the way he'd targeted the other players. The betting had puffed up Ned's sense of importance. He was winning. He'd done well. He could win this whole tournament, walk away with the wealth and capture the bad guy. A double win.

'Boss?' Jenni spoke urgently at him. 'If you make a deal in 'ere, you gotta follow it frew. Part of the magical constraints in place. I fink it's too risky. What if 'e gets away wiv it all?'

But Ned was calm. The universe had aligned within him and he could do no wrong. 'Have a little faith, Jenni.' Ned held out his hand and Armando leant forward to shake it. The watching audience booed but Jenni hushed them and gestured crossly at Gerald to get on with it.

# Chapter 16

Gerald dealt the two players their cards.

Without looking at his cards, Armando swept a hand over the table. 'All in?' he asked.

'All in,' replied Ned firmly. 'Deal them all,' he ordered the octopus as the remaining piles of gems were pushed into the centre of the table by the two players.

Gerald laid out all five cards - the nine of spades, the three of spades, the six of hearts, the ten of spades and the five of hearts.

Both men eyeballed each other challengingly.

Jenni broke the moment. 'C'mon! Get on wiv it. Show us yer cards!'

The players turned over simultaneously. Ned had the ace of clubs and the four of spades. He had nothing. He'd lost.

'No!' gasped Jenni.

The onlooking crowd echoed her disbelief.

Armando roared with laughter at the sight of Ned's cards and his own pair of tens and pair of sixes. 'Thank you very much,' he managed to say between guffaws. He clicked his fingers imperiously for a chest to put his winnings in. Jenni complied woodenly and brought the chest of gold as well, minus the ten percent for the house. The shapeshifter pulled out a small trolley from under his chair and placed both chests upon it, whistling cheerfully as he fastened them in place. It wouldn't do to lose his winnings now.

The door to the hut opened, the magical seal dissolving. Bright light spilled into the building bringing with it a zesty sea breeze and the sound of wheeling seagulls.

'Boss? What are you finking? The mermaids are gonna skin you alive for this. Not to mention Momma K. This whole fing was meant to catch 'im. You can't let 'im walk out the door.' Jenni looked desperately at her boss and took half a step towards the shapeshifter, but knew she was bound by the magical wager and could do nothing to stop him from leaving.

Ned sat back in his chair, finishing his pint, looking completely unconcerned. Mr. Simms lurched dismally out of the hut, vowing never to play poker again. Ivy and Gurgle had been busy commiserating each other; he had offered to water her roots and she'd sprouted agreeably. The two of them left together talking excitedly about the possibility of hydroponics. The spectators were unsure if there would be an awards ceremony or presentation of a certificate, so they lingered around the edges of the spectator gallery and near the open doorway. Fingers packed up and took the young barmaid with him as he left, they had another job on elsewhere in town. The octopus had already vanished.

Tipping a jaunty salute at Ned, Armando grabbed the handle of his trolley and walked to the door. His victorious exit was marred somewhat when he was unable to get the heavy chests over the lip of the doorway and out of the building. There was no one left to give him a hand except for Ned or Jenni, so Ned stood up and sauntered over. Jenni stood still in confusion, mouth open, no idea what was going on.

'Here, let me give you a hand with that.' Ned reached down and grabbed the handle of the trolley. His extra leverage helped pop the wheels over the lip and encourage the heavy winnings to leave the wooden hut.

As soon as Armando stepped fully outside the poker den, eight arms of cephalopodic menace wrapped him up tight.

'What is this? You can't arrest me, Spinks!'

Ned laughed. 'I'm not.'

Ned and Jenni had followed the shapeshifter out of the hut. Ned's magic was back, he could feel it tingling just out of reach as usual. He looked at Jenni. She flexed magically and made blue sparks dance from fingertip to fingertip. She scowled up at him.

'Wot's going on? Why is Gerald wrapping Armando up?'

It was the question on the tips of everyone's tongue. A sizeable crowd was watching the latest action unfold. They gathered near the beginning of the pier and filtered down the side, opposite the hut. Armando, Gerald, Ned and Jenni stood by themselves. Armando had managed a few steps in his struggle against tentacle arrest and was closer to the edge of the pier than the thief-catchers. They stood between him and the throng of people.

'Gerald here is on day release from Sea Precinct and is acting as an honorary thief-catcher. He is only doing his civic duty,' Ned said, folding his arms.

Armando would have complained, but the suckers on a particularly tight tentacle were preventing him from speaking at all.

'Ow did you do it though, Boss? I never seed you do nuffink.'

'Ah, well, you don't know all my secrets, Jenni.' Ned relented at the look of utter bewilderment on her face and explained. 'I happened to have a spare message in a bottle spell. It always pays to keep spares of things like that around – you taught me that. I filled it in and offered the octopus the chance to work for us.' Ned sighed. 'He was so good at the filing,' he said wistfully.

'Yeah, awright. But 'ow did you knows he would be 'ere?'

Ned tapped the side of his nose.

'No, really, Boss. 'Ow did you know?'

Ned smiled. He wasn't about to reveal his source. He didn't want to get them or him in trouble with Jenni or Momma K. 'A Chief Thief-Catcher has to have some secrets. Even from his second-in-command.'

Jenni didn't look too happy about that but she kept quiet. She reckoned it was probably Fingers anyway. He usually had a finger in every pie going, hence the nickname.

Armando sneered at them, finally managing to get his mouth partially free of sucker. 'You know this octopus is never going to hold me, right?'

From where Ned was standing, the tentacle trap looked watertight. A thought occurred to him.

'Jenni, why isn't he shifting? I thought that would be the first thing he'd do as soon as he left the building.'

It was Jenni's turn to look pleased with herself. 'Spiked his drink, didn't I. No magic in the 'ut don't mean nuffink works at all. I got a potion from the druids, they're good inna pinch. Got Fingers to put it in 'is drink when 'e ordered from the bar. Simple really.' But then she frowned. 'We gotta bind 'im soon though cos it won't last forever. I got these.' She held out spelled manacles. 'E won't be able to shift wiv these on.'

She clapped the cold irons on the indignant shifter allowing the octopus to relax his hold in places. Gerald didn't fully trust the spell or the manacles. He wasn't about to be known as the cephalopod who let a mass murderer get away.

'What do you think you are doing?' a livid voice

screamed at the collection of people on the pier. It was coming from the watery depths.

Ned shuffled closer to the side of the pier, keeping one eye on Armando. It was Pearl.

'I'm arresting the murderer.'

'You will hand him over to us. We shall deal out justice.' Her fangs were back. As were her razor-sharp claws.

Ned dithered. Part of him wanted to pass the shapeshifter over to the mermaids. He knew they could handle the retribution, but he also knew how bloody that justice was likely to be. Before he could respond, Armando took his attention.

'I wasn't always like this, you know!' shouted the shapeshifter, the first note of panic in his voice. 'It's not even my fault.'

'My arse,' scoffed Jenni but Ned shushed her.

'What do you mean? Whose fault is it?'

'I killed a fairy.'

The rapt audience gasped loudly.

'It was an irritating little thing, but it helped me realise something. Turns out I had magic of my own and could take on the appearance of others.' Armando paused for effect. Despite being immobilised, he was enjoying himself. 'It was only by killing another fae that my powers activated. You have no idea the thrill of changing your own skin. It's intoxicating.'

'That doesn't explain why your murder spree isn't your fault,' prompted Ned.

'After the fairy, I saw a centaur and thought how impressive he looked with his powerful haunches and muscular presence. The next thing I knew I had my own hooves and a tail but I didn't kill the beast and so I didn't gain his powers. I learnt about that aspect when I squished a firefly and spent the night with my own rear aglow.'

'Why I oughta...' Jenni was incensed. She was highly protective of Sparks and his many friends and relations. Her hand began to glow with the beginnings of a fireball, but Ned broke her concentration by putting his own hand over hers.

'Let him finish,' he said calmly.

'Thank you. It's quite a tale.' Armando tried to stroke his moustache with his fingers but was unable to move his hand towards his face.

'Go on,' said Ned while Jenni silently fumed.

'My next error was overdoing it.' Armando nodded towards Gurgle, the water sprite, who was watching events unfold with Ivy. 'He knows what happened there. I killed them all. Not exactly on purpose but you know what it's like when you're learning how to kill fae and steal their powers.' He searched the crowd for nods of agreement. There were none. 'Hmm. Wrong crowd I suppose. Anyway, after that massacre, it became addictive. Spend a day or two with a new species, shifting first to blend in and then killing one to take their inherent fae power. So, as I said, it's not my fault. Blame the fairy who activated my power.' For once his moustached face was earnest. He really did believe himself to be a victim of circumstance.

Before things became any more awkward, in a flash of silver light, Momma K appeared on deck to make matters even worse.

'Chil', bring him to me,' she demanded, completely ignoring Ned, the octopus, and the mermaids, speaking only to Jenni. The onlookers didn't even register with her. Momma K only had eyes for the shapeshifter. A deadly edge joined the tense atmosphere.

'Momma K, I can't. They made a deal in the 'ut. It's magically binding.' Jenni shrugged her arms, holding her palms out as if to say *what can I do*? 'But it's awight, catchers 'ave got 'im. 'E confessed to everyfink.'

'Why hasn't Momma K just taken him?' whispered Ned out of the corner of his mouth to Jenni.

'She can't. She knows the magical deal were binding. You gotta 'and 'im over willingly,' she whispered back.

Armando had stopped wiggling in his tentacle prison. The magical cuffs were beginning to burn his wrists and he was feeling the results of the druidic potion. As a rule, such potions tended to either be purging or soporific. This one was doing its best to knock the shapeshifter out. He had barely registered the appearance of Momma K.

'You can't have him, fae queen! He's our murderer – give him to us!' demanded Pearl.

'Beg to differ, fish breath!' screeched Agatha as the harpy descended in foul stench and even fouler mood. 'Hand him over to us, Spinks, and I'll rip him limb from limb.'

High-pitched squeaking let Ned know the brownies had arrived, but he was more concerned by whether the Dead Pier could take the weight of the six golem that stood on its edge. So far, none of them had ventured any further.

Jenni peered around. 'Don't see no gingerbread people. Nor pixies. Probably for the best,' she muttered. As she watched, a puddle transcended into a nixie. She gave it a little wave.

Momma K was in no mood for honouring agreements. 'Me doh care for no deal. Me didn't make no deal. Bring him here!'

The sky cracked with lightning. The onlookers

watched with interest to see who would win this battle of wills.

'Under the jurisdiction of the thief-catchers of Roshaven, we are arresting this man, er... shapeshifter, for the known murder of eight fae - ' A huge crack of thunder made Ned jump.

'Me doh accept your jurisdiction. Fae murda mean fae justice. Stand aside.'

# Chapter 17

'I will not,' said Ned firmly.

You could hear a pin drop.

'What ya say to me?' Momma K flapped her black and silver wings and ascended, so she was eye level with Ned. The two of them stared defiantly at each other.

At least, Ned tried to stare defiantly, but it was difficult when he was sure everyone could see his knees knocking together. 'By order of the Emperor - ' he began.

'MAY HE LIVE FOR EVER AND EVER' roared across the pier from the riveted audience. Runners must have been sent to the other inhabitants of Roshaven, for the crowd was growing. No one wanted to miss anything. The pier creaked and groaned under the increasing weight.

Trying not to think about the structural integrity of the Dead Pier, Ned took a little courage from the supportive crowd and rallied. 'It is the duty of the office of thief-catcher to apprehend and bring to justice all thieves, murderers and persons of an unsavoury nature wherever and whenever a crime is committed upon the imperial soil of Roshaven.'

You could hear two pin drops.

'Fae law states a fae break de rule, a fae pay. It written in blood. It bindin' to de soul.' Momma K's voice rang out across the pier and seemed to have its own echo as it danced off bony decking and reverberated through the spectator crowd.

'You promised us vengeance!' Pearl shouted from the water.

'Give him to Momma K,' hissed Agatha now taking her queen's side, figuring she'd let the harpies deal their own brand of murderous justice.

Ned risked another sideways glance to the sea and saw that more merpeople had joined Pearl. The waters were beginning to churn.

Taking the initiative, Momma K tried another tack. 'My way get vengeance.' She gestured toward Ned. 'Him way get you nott'ing.'

Ned tried to think of a suitable comeback but was interrupted by a loud rattling noise coming from the direction of dry land. The crowd parted rapidly and a large imperial carriage, pulled by four white horses, clattered onto the Dead Pier, each hoof making a sickening clop upon the surface.

The carriage, outfitted in imperial purple and gold, came to a stop. The crowd could hear running footsteps in the distance getting closer, so they waited patiently to see what would happen next. Momma K tutted loudly at the interruption.

Finally, Fred, the young palace guard, wheezed into view. He had been running as fast as he could in full ceremonial garb, carrying the emperor's standard and of course, his plumed helmet. 'I fell off! Left me behind! Tried to catch up!' he gasped as he reached the carriage then put his hands on his knees and blew hard for a moment, trying to get his breath. 'I'm supposed to do the announcing!'

'You can do it now, if you like,' Ned said, grateful for a way to ease the tension between himself and Momma K.

Fred held up one finger and continued to pant loudly. There was no movement from the imperial coach.

'Whenever you're ready,' prompted Ned.

Fred pushed himself to standing, using the standard for support, and jammed his helmet back on his head. It teetered impressively.

'His eminence, the Emperor of Roshaven!' declared Fred, one arm flung towards the carriage.

'MAY HE LIVE FOR EVER AND EVER.' Again, the crowd joined in.

'Jus' because ya leada is here, doh mean ya won de right to justice,' hissed Momma K.

Armando had recovered his senses somewhat and was doing his best to wriggle out of the tentacle grip. Fred wandered over to take a closer look at the captured criminal while Momma K and Ned began to glare at each other once more.

Fred leaned forward slightly to inspect the prisoner. 'So, you're the wanted man, then? Huh. I thought moustaches went out ages ago. Our Brian says he wouldn't be seen dead with one.' Fred grinned at the trussed-up murderer who finally managed to get one up on the octopus and pushed an arm out of his restraints.

Armando's fist punched Fred without any of its intended malice. There wasn't enough force to bruise the guard's delicate personage, but it was enough to shift Fred's balance and topple the already precarious helmet from his head onto the decking.

Ned, Momma K, Fred and all the spectators watched in slow motion as the helmet rolled towards Armando and Gerald who were still wrestling and completely oblivious to the moving headgear.

'What's going on? Why has it gone quiet?' shouted Pearl.

'Fred's lost 'is 'elmet,' explained Jenni helpfully.

'Who the crevice is Fred?'

But this time, no one answered the mermaid. All eyes were glued on Fred's plumed helmet. As Armando lifted one leg to try and gain some momentum against a tiny amount of give in Gerald's grip, the helmet lazily rolled beneath his foot. Instead of stepping down onto the deck of the pier, Armando's boot reeled off the helmet, causing him to lose his footing completely and send him arm-wheeling backwards. At least, he would have been arm-wheeling if his arms were free. As it was, Gerald swayed violently, trying to keep his tentacles around the shapeshifter and failing miserably. Armando managed to throw the octopus free and Gerald landed with a slap on the decking. Everyone watched in sick fascination as Armando continued to stagger backwards, his balance even more unsteady after losing the cephalopod counterweight. His legs banged into his chest of winnings, causing him to trip over the wealth and fall fully backwards, missing the pier all together and landing with an enormous splash in the vampire mermaid infested waters below.

# Chapter 18

The water boiled as fins flashed and merpeople fought to each get their own pound of flesh. Jenni walked to the edge of the pier and watched in gruesome fascination with Momma K hovering at her shoulder. Ned felt it was his duty to uphold Roshaven law and bear witness to the slaughter, but his stomach was vehemently against the idea. The crowd had no such compunction and rushed to watch the shapeshifter's grisly end.

'Jenni!' Ned yelled in slight panic at the approaching mob.

She didn't even turn around. Instead, she waggled her fingers behind her back and a crime scene protector bubble, regularly used by the thief-catchers, descended around Ned, Momma K, Jenni, Gerald and the shell-shocked Fred.

Ned watched as the fastest gawkers bounced off the shield. Thankfully, sound was muted, although he could guess what some of the more aggressive gestures meant. Forgetting himself for a moment, Ned walked closer to the edge of the pier and caught sight of the remains of the shapeshifter in the water below. There were a few scraps of blood-stained white linen floating here and there between the frequent flashes of tail and fin that churned the water, now boiling with red-tinged bubbles. Ned's stomach wobbled. He chose instead to check on Fred.

'Are you okay?' Ned asked kindly, one hand patting Fred on the shoulder.

'I never - I mean - I didn't, because I'd never - you

know - it was an accident.' He looked up at Ned with an ashen face. 'These helmets never fit my head properly, no matter what I do.' He cast a fearful glance towards the ocean. 'Will I get into trouble, Mr. Spinks? Have you got to arrest me now? I'll come willingly. Only I need to make sure our Brian looks after everything because... you know how he is with things. Doesn't know if he's coming or going most of the time.' Fred sniffed; his eyes full of tears.

Before Ned could reply, Momma K spoke to the young guard.

'You gave fae dere justice. You did good, boy. A pure soul always shines true.' She wore a very satisfied expression on her face. 'Dis will do for him crimes. Dis will do.'

'So, I won't be arrested?' Fred asked hopefully.

'Me no press charges.' Momma K made a pushing motion with her arms and Jenni's bubble disintegrated. 'Anyone here tink de boy did wrong?'

There was a moment of silence, then the crowd erupted in enthusiastic agreement, that *de boy* had done no wrong at all, and everything was at it should be.

Fred sat straighter and gave a tentative smile.

Ned clapped him on the shoulder again then walked towards the emperor's carriage. 'We should find out what His Eminence thinks about all this.' Ned rapped his knuckles on the carriage door, but there was no reply. He knocked again, harder this time. Still no response. Feeling all eyes on him, Ned gripped the handle of the carriage and opened it cautiously. There was nobody inside.

'You had a dirty deal, didn't you?' Ned swung round and accused Momma K hotly. 'You knew it would come down to some kind of bloodthirsty destruction. All this...'

He waved his hands in the air manically. 'All this was for nothing, wasn't it? The game, the hut. Everything was just a show. A build up for you getting your own way.' He stopped, breathing heavily. He had lots more to say, but Jenni had grabbed his arm and was begging Ned with her eyes to shut up before he got himself into any more trouble. He shook her off. 'I get it. You did your deal behind closed doors and that empty carriage came because the emperor wanted to be seen to have witnessed justice. Well, I'll tell you something.' He pointed angrily at the water. 'That is not my justice.'

The carriage door fell shut, and the vehicle began to clatter away, responding to some unseen signal. Fred clambered to his feet, dropped his helmet twice and scrabbled to pick up the emperor's standard before rushing after the carriage.

'Wait! Wait for me. I'm supposed to be on that. Wait!' he yelled, giving Ned an apologetic look as he dashed past.

Momma K fluttered over to Ned and poked him in the chest. He winced. She had very hard fingers.

'Justice has been done. Dat is de important ting 'ere.' She cast a disapproving glare at her daughter then looked Ned up and down before poking him again. 'Dis office you stand for, it have a good heart. See dat it stay dat way.' Her final poke made Ned stagger back slightly. He rubbed his chest, wincing.

Momma K hadn't finished with Jenni. She landed on the pier with a delicate tap. 'Sooner later chil', ya gonna have to choose. Dat choice will be hardest ting ya ever face. I doh feel ya know where ya belong but ya heart is fae. Always fae. Rememba dat.'

Ned blinked, and Momma K was not there anymore. There was a slight crackle in the air suggesting the use of great power. Unlike Jenni, who had a greasy popping sound when she appeared and disappeared, Momma K had ceased to exist in that particular time and space. Jenni licked her finger, touched one of the crackles, then sucked her finger rapidly, muttering to herself.

'You alright?' asked Ned.

'Yeah.'

'We'd better clear this pier then, I guess.'

Jenni turned, standing on her boss's boot affectionately, then cupped her hands around her mouth and yelled. 'Awright you 'orrible lot. Beat it. Show's over. Go 'ome, get out of 'ere. There's nuffink going on no more.' She winked at the crowd. 'We'll see you at the next one!'

****

# How To Play Poker by Jenni

The type of poker wot is being played in this book is called Texas Hold 'Em. It's a very poplar type of poker played in lots of dimensions including yours. 'Ere are some of the rules and what they mean, in case you ain't never played poker afore.

When the game starts the dealer tells you wot the blinds is. There's a big 'un and a little 'un. The player to the left of the dealer does the little, the one next to 'im does the big, then it moves round the table each round. As the game goes on the blinds usually go up. It raises the stakes.

In the beginning the dealer will give every player two cards. He deals 'em face down which means no one can see wot they is. But you is allowed to look at your cards. Once everyone has their cards there is a round of betting. You gotta try and figure out if your cards are any good. There are four fings wot you can do:

Check – do nuffink (and 'ope no one else does nuffink)
Bet – frow in some jools or gold bits or whatever it is you're betting wiv
Raise – bet more than you 'ave to
Fold – quit cos your cards ain't no good

If you check and someone else bets, you gotta match their bet to stay in the game. Ovverwise you gotta fold.

Once all the players have finished sorting out what they're doing, the dealer deals a novver three cards. This time everyone can see their faces. They go in the middle of the table and they're part of your 'and. If you wants 'em.

A 'and is wot you call the cards you 'ave.

Once the three cards go down there's a novver round of betting. Same rules apply – check, bet, raise or fold. If you check and some one else bets and you decide you can't match it, you lose wot jools, gold bits or whatever you've already bet. Thems the rules.

Dealer puts a novver card in the middle. This is 'is fourth.

Then you gotta bet, again.

Then the last card comes in. Oh, and one more lot of betting.

You can only win wiv five cards and you 'ave the choice of using the two wot you got at the beginning plus any three from the middle, or one of yours and four of them or even just the five in the middle if they're real good. You can't swap cards wiv no one else, even if you really wants to.

Usually, the player wot has the best hand wins the pot. But sometimes someone will bet so much that everyone else folds cos they're all psyched out by it and stuffs. So, if you can 'timidate people then you might be good at poker. You don't 'ave to 'ave the best 'and to win.

'Ere are some splanations of winning 'ands and stuff.

## All-in
This is wot you say when you're betting all your jools. Or gold bits. Or whatever.

## Big Blind
This is double the small 'un. It's a fixed bet wot you 'ave to play in order to start the round. No 'ceptions.

## Bluff
This is wot you do if you ain't got no good cards but you reckon you can fake it wiv all the uvver players and psyche 'em all out so you keep betting.

## Buy-in
This is wot you pay so you can play. No refunds.

## Check
This is wot you do when it's your go and you don't wanna bet.

## Flush
This is five cards of the same suit so like, five 'earts or five spades. This can be a winning 'and.

## Fold
This is wot you do when you quit the round.

## Four of a kind
This is when you 'ave four cards with same number so like, four nines or four queens or whatever.

**Full 'ouse**

This is when you have three cards wot are the same plus two cards wot are the same so like, three aces and two queens.

**High Card**

This is when no one has nuffink but there has to be a winner so 'ighest card wins.

**Pot**

This is the amount of moolah on the table wot you can win.

**Raise**

This is when you bet 'igher than you 'ave to, adding more to the pot.

**Royal Flush**

This is the best 'and you can get. It's Ace-King-Queen-Jack-10 all from the same suit so like, all 'earts or all diamonds.

**Small blind**

This is the little bet wot is put in the pot afore the game starts. You 'ave to do this. Thems the rules.

**Straight**

This is when you got five consec, conseccy, consessy… when you got five cards wot go one after the uvver. But they can be any suit so like, two of clubs then three of 'earts then four of clubs then five of diamonds then six of spades. Or whatever.

**Straight Flush**
This is when you got five cards wot come after each other but they is all the same suit so like, the two, three, four, five and six of 'earts. Or whatever.

**Three Of A Kind**
This is when you 'ave three cards wot are the same so like, three jacks or three threes or whatever.

**Two Of A Kind**
This is when you 'ave two cards wot are the same so like, two queens or two twos or whatever.

**Two Pair**
This is when you 'ave two lots of two cards wot are the same so like, two tens and two kings or whatever.

So there you 'ave it, yor guide on 'ow to play poker. It ain't all that tricksy, just make sure you never bet everyfink you 'ave cos if you do lose then you won't have nuffink left and that'd be daft. Best to play with beetles or summik I reckon.

Keep yor eyes peeled for a nuvver fing like this. I reckon I'm good at splaining.

Cheers, Jenni.

# About the Author

Claire Buss is a multi-genre author and poet based in the UK. She wanted to be Lois Lane when she grew up but work experience at her local paper was eye-opening. Instead, Claire went on to work in a variety of admin roles for over a decade but never felt quite at home. An avid reader, baker and Pinterest addict Claire won second place in the Barking and Dagenham Pen to Print writing competition in 2015 with her debut novel, The Gaia Effect, setting her writing career in motion. She continues to write passionately and is hopelessly addicted to cake.

Sign up for her newsletter at http://eepurl.com/c93M2L

# The Rose Thief by Claire Buss

Ned Spinks, Chief Thief-Catcher has a problem. Someone is stealing the Emperor's roses. But that's not the worst of it. In his infinite wisdom and grace, the Emperor magically imbued his red rose with love so if it was ever removed from the Imperial Rose Gardens then love will be lost, to everyone, forever. It's up to Ned and his band of motley catchers to apprehend the thief and save the day. But the thief isn't exactly who they seem to be, neither is the Emperor. Ned and his team will have to go on a quest defeating vampire mermaids, illusionists, estranged family members and an evil sorcerer in order to win the day. What could possibly go wrong?

Available to buy in paperback and eBook at https://books2read.com/u/bQaxw6

Read the first chapter here:

# Chapter 1

He, or very possibly she, was known as The Rose Thief. It was a nickname that stuck despite the best efforts of the thief-catchers to stem public approval for a thief who only stole roses. No-one had yet admitted to knowing who, or indeed what, the thief was. He could indeed be a woman, or a troll, or even a malevolent spirit. What was of great significance and importance was that only the Emperor's – *may he live for ever and ever* – rose garden was being violated.

The thief was stealing exclusively from the Emperor – *may he live for ever and ever* – and no-one but the Emperor – *may he, oh you get the idea* – had access to the rose gardens. Not even any of his thousand and one wives. It made solving the theft extremely difficult.

It also made the Emperor look rather foolish and was the reason why Chief Thief-Catcher, Ned Spinks, was strung up by his ankles, in the third best reception room of the Emperor's Palace.

Ned was waiting to see what would happen next, and to amuse himself in the meantime, was tracing rude shapes in his imagination with the dark stains on the floor beneath him.

'Do you know why you are here?'

The high-pitched, nasal voice came from the direction of Ned's right knee. It was the High Right, the Honourable Lord Chamberlain. Ned tried to swing around a little so he could at least speak to the ankles of the High Right, but he had no turning circle. The blood pooling in his head was beginning to make it hard to think coherently. He decided against his usual witty repartee.

'It's my turn?' Well, maybe just a little. To lighten the mood.

The High Right ignored Ned's response. 'The Emperor – *may he live for ever and ever* – wants this so-called *Thief of Roses* caught. Now.'

'I'll see what I can do, Sir.'

The High Right did not respond and remained behind Ned, making him uneasy.

Due to the voluminous nature of his shirt, a large portion of Ned's back was on display and he didn't think it was necessarily his best side. Feeling rather vulnerable, he was now thoroughly convinced that love handles were not meant to sag upside down. Gravity was not doing him any favours.

He lurched unexpectedly as he was cut down and crashed to the floor in an inelegant heap of slightly overweight thief-catcher. Shaking the stars from his head, Ned winced as the blood rushed back down his body and made his ears ring. At least he still had his ears. The last time the Emperor took a dislike to the Chief Thief-Catcher, the High Left Inquisitor carved most of his body parts off. Ned counted his fingers and toes surreptitiously.

'You have one day, Thief-Catcher.' The High Right glared at Ned who had reached a count of at least eight digits. 'Don't let me regret not ordering the removal of your eyeballs.'

Ned heard rather than saw the High Right leave.

His head was still adjusting to being the right way up and despite the leg count, Ned wasn't entirely sure he had active control over his limbs. Standing had yet to be attempted.

A rather loud conversation began filtering through the third best reception room doors, which were ajar.

'I don't care what you fink. I'm going in to get 'im.'

A small, grubby looking child with a mop of straw-like hair marched into the room wearing an air of nonchalance which soon deflated into obvious relief at seeing Ned in one piece. Two Palace Guards peered in, saw that the High Right had finished and decided to mind their own business for once. Palace Guards excelled at minding yours, it was a strenuous part of training: you couldn't be a Palace Guard if you didn't know what your nextdoor neighbour's aunt had for tea last Thursday.

The small child wasn't a child at all. She was a dirty little sprite with large, hairy ears and a coppery coloured tail just visible from the bottom of her filthy red coat. She peered into Ned's face.

The smell that accompanied her was other-worldly.

'Jenni. A little space.' Ned tried not to breathe.

Jenni huffed, hurt at the not so warm welcome. 'Be like that then. I only came straight 'ere to find you and get you out of whatever mess you're in now.' She leaned in again, utterly disregarding Ned's request for personal space, and looked deep into the bloodshot yet still vibrant blue eyes of her boss. 'Joe said you was scooped.'

Ned pushed himself up from the floor, trying in vain to ignore the incredible smell infiltrating his nostrils. 'Yep. Lucky me.' He staggered a few steps before collecting his limbs and walking towards the door. Jenni capered at his side. 'You need a bath, Jenni. You stink.'

'Been undercover at the docks, ain't I?' A few flies buzzed in Jenni's wake. 'Cos we fawt he might be basing 'is operations round that way, right? So I've bin looking for the rose thief, ain't I?' She scratched an armpit viciously. 'Came straight 'ere tho di'n't I? When Joe said.'

'Yeah, thanks. What about the docks, what did you find out?' Ned held the third best reception room door open for Jenni and jauntily saluted the guards in the corridor as they walked through. 'Any luck?'

'Just a pile o' shite.'

'Well, I can smell that.'

'Nah, a proper pile of rose shite – that special stuff what makes them grow.' Jenni jabbed her thumb over her shoulder at the Palace receding behind them as they exited through a side gate. 'And it ain't theirs.'

'Whose was it then?'

'Dunno. Didn't 'zactly speak to the owner. There weren't much left, right, and it was in one of them hire when you need a bit o' space like places. You know, the ones Two-Face Bob hires out. It'd dried a bit and that, but it was definitely shite.' She beamed up at Ned. 'So even though I di'n't find nobody, I still done good, right?'

Ned nodded, then winced as his upside-down headache kicked in. 'Could be Two-Face Bob is involved, we'll have to have a little chat with him.' He tried to make a mental note to investigate the dockyards further whilst ignoring the hammers in his head.

The unlikely pair walked down Palace Lane, back to Headquarters at The Noose. They did not notice the wide berth the great unwashed gave them, which goes to show that even the down and outs in Roshaven have some standards.

Headquarters wasn't the real headquarters. The official residence of the thief-catchers, over on Justice Heights, burned down in '04 after a nasty disagreement with the Guild of Organised Flame.

It was rebuilt twice before the then Chief Thief-Catcher took the hint and upped sticks.

These days anyone who wanted to find a thief-catcher visited The Noose, a delightful little hostelry that perched jauntily on the edge of the aptly named Black Narrows.

If by delightful you meant grime encrusted walls, floors and ceiling; a barman who'd sooner shoot you than serve you; and a clientele that lacked a certain respectability; then yes, The Noose was extremely delightful. As for the Black Narrows, they were definitely black. Some say it was because that was the only colour of stone left in the quarry, others say it's because all the evil committed in the narrows had stained the streets with blackness. And they were certainly narrow. So narrow, they were a pickpockets' dream. No-one went into the Black Narrows voluntarily, unless they were naive tourists or had the misfortune to live there. And if you did live there, no-one went out in the narrows at night unless they absolutely had to and even then they tried to get out of it. Of course, for some, it was part of their professional workload to be in the narrows, especially at night. It was one of *those* places, a tourist honey trap for people seeking danger, and suitable living conditions for those wishing to cause the danger. All in all, it was the perfect location for Thief-Catcher HQ. Anyone who was that serious about needing a thief-catcher clearly had the funds for the job and no-one, not even the Guild of Organised Flame, was brave enough to try and destroy The Noose. They'd rather be hung, drawn and quartered.

Reg, The Noose's resident barman - he never, ever, left - nodded in greeting as Ned entered through the concealed side door. It was the shortest route to the rickety stairs that lurked in the rear of the saloon where the gloom was deepest, knee high and thick as treacle in places.

'Anything?' Ned asked. Reg acted as a surly doorman for the thief-catchers, he let everyone in, regardless of whether they were welcome or not, but he was supposed to let Ned know in advance if he let people through when no-one was around. Especially anyone connected with the current Rose Thief investigations.

'Up.' Reg didn't believe in conversation or indeed sentences with more than one word. They were unhealthy and contagious.

The Noose's patrons were of a similar mind except on Thursdays when Yvette von Strunkle performed her weekly show. Then many rich and colourful words were shouted, often hoarsely, by short, hairy men in large overcoats who brought their own peanuts and drank copious amounts of the vilest liquor available.

Ned nodded his thanks and began the treacherous climb. One in five steps were missing and those that remained were so old and rotten that putting any weight on them was risking a broken limb. Ned tried to look at it as a deterrent for time wasters. You had to really want the thief-catchers to climb these stairs. As they skirted the mattress at the top of the stairs, Ned noticed the door to the thief-catcher office was ajar, a shadowy figure visible through the frosted glass. Ned put an arm out to slow Jenni down and went first, a catch spell on quick release from the supply in his spell-caster belt. As soon as he saw who it was he relaxed.

Bob's two noses wrinkled as Jenni's fragrance filled the office.

The sprite stood behind Bob and stuck her tongue out rudely. The face on the back of Bob's head retaliated by hawking and spitting snotty phlegm at the sprite. She dodged it easily and began to make one of her own.

'Jenni, enough.' Ned plonked himself down wearily in the nearest chair. 'Two-Face Bob, what can I do for you?'

Both faces smirked and spoke in unison. 'It's not what you can do for me, Spinks, it's what I can do for you. For a price.'

'And that is?'

'I know who the Rose Thief is.'

'Yeah?' scoffed Jenni. 'Wot you got stinking in your warehouse by the dock then, eh? We know all about that an' all.'

'Jenni!' Ned leaned back in his chair, putting his battered boots up on the corner of his battered desk before responding to Two-Face. 'Why come to me? Why not report it to the Palace yourself.'

Two-Face Bob walked over to the small window and peered out, looking up and down the street below before turning back to Ned and rubbing his hands.

'Pay me first. Then I'll tell you everything I know. This is a big one right – at least four thousand gold bits.'

'Ha! Four thousand gold... you must be joking. Not even the Emperor has that kind of cash just lying around.'

'*May he live for ever and ever*,' whispered the rear head of Two-Face Bob.

'We already know it's you anyways – what yer talking about bits? You ain't getting no bits.' said Jenni but Two-Face Bob ignored her.

'I know you got scooped up and I know you've got a deadline.' He jerked a thumb over his shoulder at the sprite who was picking her nails in disinterest. 'I doubt the pixie will be much help to you.'

'Sprite.' Ned corrected him.

'What?'

'She's a sprite and unless you have any hard evidence you'd like to leave with the thief-catchers office, get out of my sight.'

Two-Face Bob turned so that his faces could scowl at both Ned and Jenni before he stalked out of the room and banged the door shut.

'Four thousand gold bits.' Ned shook his head. 'You believe that guy?' Moving his head was a bad idea, it reawakened the killer headache he'd been trying to ignore, and Jenni's stink was starting to make his eyes water again. 'You, go get clean. Come straight back and fill me in again on what you found.' He pulled open the drawers of his desk, searching for something, anything that would clear his head. He opted for the half bottle of scrumble he'd been saving for a rainy day.

Jenni clattered and banged in the small bathroom next door while Ned reviewed the case so far.

****